Deadly Curse

ANGUS BRODIE AND MIKAELA FORSYTHE MURDER MYSTERY
BOOK ELEVEN

CARLA SIMPSON

Cover art by Dar Albert at Wicked Smart Designs

Published by Oliver-Heber Books

0 9 8 7 6 5 4 3 2 1

One

SPRING HAD AT LAST MADE an appearance across London. We'd now had sunshine three days in a row!

It was a record to be certain according to my great aunt, Lady Antonia Montgomery, as Mr. Hastings, her driver, maneuvered the coach through early morning traffic toward the British Museum.

Mr. Munro had convinced her to take the coach with the weather uncertain—he was after all a Scot, as well as her manager of estates and current caretaker of the open motor carriage she had purchased.

He knew a little about weather, that it could be *stuamachd*, he had explained in that broad Scots accent.

"Temperamental," Brodie had translated as Mr. Hastings had arrived at the townhouse in Mayfair.

"A bit like a woman," he added as he set off with the cabman who had arrived to take him to the office on the Strand and a meeting the current *acting* Chief Inspector of Police had requested.

I was immediately suspicious. There was no love lost by

either of us when it came to the Metropolitan Police and past incidents. The most grievous, however, had been the actions of Chief Inspector Abberline, who had Brodie arrested and imprisoned under false charges in retaliation for a past incident when Brodie was an inspector with the MET.

If not for the intervention of Sir Avery Stanton of the Special Services Agency, he might have been hanged. Or in the very least, sent to Newgate.

Abberline—I refused to acknowledge him with any accolade—he was presently on *indefinite leave* over the matter. Interim Chief Inspector Graham was a man Brodie had served with and respected.

The *indefinite* part of Abberline's departure should be *definite*, as far as I was concerned. He simply was not to be trusted, and I for one did not accept the formal apology he had made to Brodie over the whole affair. An old saying came to mind: leopards did not change their spots.

The weather did behave itself, as my great aunt commented, as we arrived at the museum. I didn't bother to mention the clouds that steadily rolled in from the Thames.

Instead, I tucked both our umbrellas under my arm as we disembarked the coach at the main entrance, with those tall columns at either side and the overhead banner spread between that announced the opening of the newest addition to the Egyptian wing.

"Do ye want me to come with ye?" Munro asked as I slipped my other arm under my great aunt's—not that she needed assistance.

She was hale and hearty and would undoubtedly outlive us all. However, she had taken to using a walking cane the past year after an "undesirable encounter," as she put it.

It wasn't as if she needed the cane for assistance with walking. However, it made an excellent weapon.

"Not at all, Mr. Munro," she informed him as she tapped her way ahead. "It is not as if there is anything dangerous or life threatening in an exhibit of ancient relics and artifacts, not to mention a few dead people."

Sarcophagi was more accurate, complete with the remains of mummies that had been publicized over the past several weeks as the exhibit approached completion.

"Aye," Munro replied as he returned to the coach. "Mr. Hastings will return by the noon hour."

"Do come along, Mikaela," my great aunt said as she climbed the steps ahead unassisted. "This is most exciting."

I caught up with her inside the main entrance. We followed other attendees to the Egyptian hall.

"I don't believe I mentioned that I once entertained Sir Nelson's father," she added conversationally. "Quite handsome, but also quite the philanderer. However, we remained good friends."

Entertained? Knowing my great aunt, that might include almost anything. I did not ask.

She had never married, although it seemed there had been no shortage of suitors when she was a young woman. As she explained it, she had simply never found a man worth giving up her single status, particularly as her father's heir to the Montgomery estates.

"That whole thing about all my properties and possessions passing on to a husband," she once said. "I never found one worth my time, let alone the family fortune. And it isn't as if I don't have a family of my own."

As for having once entertained Sir Nelson's father?

"Only once," she explained now, which was more than I

cared to know, as we approached the hall where the Egyptian room was located.

"That was enough. The man was quite inept."

I did not inquire what that might mean.

With my great aunt safely escorted to the exhibit hall for the new Egyptian exhibit, I continued on to the office of Sir Nelson Lawrence, who was responsible for discovering the artifacts and then bringing them to London for the exhibit.

We had met previously when I was on an early adventure to Egypt while he was on his latest exploration and was to be spending the next several months there.

In recent years he had established himself as an authority on Egypt, its history and culture, and had brought back countless artifacts, including the present exhibit.

He was highly educated, and had spent almost twenty years in Egypt, yet not the usual sort one might expect ... distracted, and somewhat aloof.

Instead, he had been most congenial, not at all put off by my endless questions, and even extended an invitation to visit the site he was returning to, to continue his work.

During that long voyage when we first met, he had taken on the unofficial position of travel guide, and continued once we reached Cairo for the handful of us who chose to venture into the Valley of the Kings.

He had written me several times after my return, and I found his updates on his latest pursuits fascinating. He had also written me before this latest return, along with a description of the artifacts he was bringing with him. I was looking forward to the exhibit, and eager to see him again and learn more about his recent travels.

His assistant, Mr. Hosni, informed me that he had already

gone to the new room where the exhibit was to open that morning.

"You might find him there," he explained in perfect Queen's English.

We had not met before, but Sir Nelson had spoken highly of Mr. Hosni. He had been educated in London, and returned to Cairo with Sir Nelson on a previous trip and had been with him since.

He was soft-spoken, slender of stature, and wore a conventional suit, as I had seen many wearing when I was in Cairo, along with a turban. His beard was neatly trimmed, and that dark gaze reminded me of another. Yet there was a distinct difference in his hooded expression.

I thanked him and returned to the hallway outside the new exhibit room.

Guests had gathered in the saloon across from the room with the new exhibits.

"Good heavens!" my great aunt whispered as I rejoined her. "There is Louisa Ivers-Braithwaite. I thought she was dead and I had simply missed the announcement in the dailies. She might as well be, she doesn't look at all well."

Aunt Antonia did have a habit of speaking quite bluntly. She had once explained that at her age, she simply didn't have time for proper social exchanges. She therefore had a tendency to be quite outspoken.

It did seem that Louisa Ivers-Braithwaite was intent on giving more than a mere nod in greeting, as she started toward us through the crowd as we waited for the exhibit to open.

I quickly removed myself and made for the refreshment banquet for a cup of coffee. I could only guess at their conversation as I watched their exchange.

As for Louisa Ivers-Braithwaite's response to a comment from my great aunt, "Oh, my!"

I could only guess by the expression on her face, which suddenly changed to wide-eyed surprise and shock, as what little color she had drained from her face.

They were both saved any further exchange or shock, as a docent of the museum appeared at the entrance to the saloon and announced that the exhibit was now open.

"How is Mrs. Ivers-Braithwaite?" I inquired as I joined my great aunt.

"A dithering idiot. I am convinced that the world is a much safer place without her son adding to the population. I saw him not long ago. Put a gown and wig on him and one would not be able to tell them apart."

We crossed the hallway to the entrance of the Egyptian Room and presented our embossed invitations to the docent. We followed the queue of visitors into the room, where we were greeted by young Mr. Howard Carter, whom I had met on previous explorations of the museum.

"I was hoping you would attend, Lady Forsythe," he greeted me. "Knowing of your previous travel to Egypt, of course."

We exchanged greetings, and I introduced my great aunt.

Although barely twenty years old, Mr. Carter had finally secured a position with the museum and planned to accompany Sir Nelson when he returned to Egypt.

"The exhibit is quite magnificent," he commented. "I was able to assist in preparing it for today's opening. I just returned from the museum director's office. Do let me know if I can be of any help, or answer any questions."

And he was off to make his rounds of the guests.

"Do let us see what Sir Nelson has brought back this time,"

my great aunt commented. "Always fascinating to view the arti-facts of other cultures. This should cause quite a stir with Sir William Flinders Petrie. Until now, he has been considered the foremost expert in Egyptian antiquities."

I was aware of Sir William's exhibitions over the past few years. He had acquired substantial backing for his ventures to Egypt and had presented those exhibitions in the Edward Library at the University College.

A rivalry between the two men had been promoted in the newspapers, and the invitation my great aunt had received spoke to that rivalry, promoting Sir Nelson's exhibit as possessing the most extensive and important discoveries to be found in Egypt to date.

To say the exhibit was magnificent, was an understatement. Carved stone busts of ancient figures filled at least a dozen glass display cases, while a half-dozen enormous carved statues lined the walls between floor-to-ceiling columns. The craftsmanship, over two thousand years old, was remarkable.

Glass cases displayed a variety of ancient tools and weapons down the center of the room, each one with a label that described where it had been found and the purpose for it. Between each set of cases were ancient figures of animals on pedestals, representing various Egyptian gods that included two lion-headed goddess statues of Sakhmet, a bronze figure of a cat, the sacred animal of the goddess Bastet, and a statue of a jackal that represented Anubis, protector of the dead.

However, the central figure of the exhibit was a towering statue of Ramses II at the far end of the room.

As we awaited the arrival of Sir Nelson, the man respon-sible for bringing the magnificent exhibit to London, I stopped to admire a glass case with finely made tools and instruments.

Some were claimed to have been used for surgical procedures according to the placard inside the cabinet.

I had learned in my travels that the Egyptians were fascinated with exploring the human body, which undoubtedly had led to the removal of human organs found in canopic jars. They had performed complicated medical procedures as well, according to ancient papyruses that had been discovered, including surgeries of the brain.

They were considerably more advanced than some of those who practiced what was referred to as modern medicine, excluding Mr. Brimley, of course, who had assisted Brodie and me in several of our inquiry cases.

We had been waiting for some time for Sir Nelson to join the exhibition, which seemed odd since Mr. Hosni had told me that he had already arrived for the new exhibit.

Always content to go exploring about on her own, my great aunt continued on ahead in the direction of the statue of Ramses II, when I suddenly heard her startled exclamation.

"Good heavens!"

My first thought was that it might have been another encounter with Louisa Ivers-Braithwaite, although I was quite confident she could handle the woman. And truth was, her exclamation was not one of impatience, but that of someone genuinely startled. And there was hardly anything that startled my great aunt.

Had she perhaps been taken with a health episode? At her age it would not have been unusual. Yet, this was my great aunt, who I was certain would live for at least another hundred years.

I rounded a display with a statue of Osiris, protector of the dead, as I heard a scream and, as I reached that impressive floor-to-ceiling statue of Ramses II, found Aunt Antonia comforting a woman who appeared as if she might faint at any moment.

It took me a moment to determine what had caused both women's reactions. Then I saw the body that lay at the feet of the statue.

Blood stained the front of the man's shirt, where a gold-handled knife protruded from a wound in his chest, and a vividly painted Egyptian funerary mask covered his face.

"I must say, not something one sees every day," Aunt Antonia commented as shouts of alarm and other screams went out across the gallery as a crowd gathered.

I knelt beside the body and carefully removed the mask.

Sir Nelson Lawrence was very dead.

Two

I HAVE DISCOVERED that people usually display two types of reactions to such situations.

The first one is shock and then horror at the sight of a body, not to mention a great deal of blood. And then there was my reaction, most usually that of curiosity.

Brodie was convinced there was something most unusual about me in that regard. Something that made me curious rather than terrified, with a penchant for asking questions and making notes that often ended up in one of my novels.

And speaking of Brodie ...

As the alarm had been raised about the discovery of the body of Sir Nelson, the room had been sealed off and the authorities contacted. Everyone was asked to remain, not that we could have escaped with the doors closed.

Several uniformed constables arrived, along with someone I knew quite well, Mr. Dooley, recently promoted to inspector with the Metropolitan Police.

Everyone in the hall had been ushered to the opposite end of the room. Names were taken to be checked against the guest list. And then Brodie arrived, no doubt made aware of our situation by Mr. Munro, who, it seemed, had returned earlier than expected.

Brodie had once worked with Mr. Dooley when both were with the MET. After Brodie's departure, Mr. Dooley had assisted, discreetly, in our various inquiry cases.

Due to that prior service and Mr. Dooley's respect for Brodie, he was allowed to enter the room and immediately made his way to where my I sat with pen and notebook in hand. That dark gaze narrowed as he found me.

"I received word," he said, reaching out. "Are ye all right?" He then answered his own question. "Well enough, I can see."

That frown slowly disappeared. "And her ladyship?" he then asked, that gaze scanning the other guests in that way of the police inspector he had once been. There were some things that never changed.

"She is presently organizing refreshments for everyone, since we are being detained," I replied. My great aunt *was* an accomplished hostess of the first order.

Her most recent endeavor had been the Christmas holiday reception at her home at Sussex Square for over two hundred guests. Presently at the museum, she had commandeered Mr. Howard, three other museum staff, and an equal number of police constables to bring coffee and sandwiches from the saloon across the hall for those presently restricted to the scene of the crime.

"Here you are, Mr. Brodie," she greeted him as she swept toward us, tap-tapping her way much like a field general commanding an army.

"It does seem as if you and Mikaela might have a new inquiry case," she commented. "Poor man murdered right in the middle of his exhibition, and with one of the artifacts from the collection."

Her eyes sparkled. Not what one might have expected from an eighty-six-year-old woman who had been the first person to discover the body, and a rather bloody one at that.

Mr. Dooley greeted us, then acknowledged my great aunt as he approached. "A most serious situation," he looked over at me. "You do seem to have a way of finding yerself in the middle of a crime, Miss Forsythe."

"Merely a guest at the opening of the new exhibit, I assure you Mr. Dooley," I replied. "However, I do have notes I've made about my great aunt's discovery of the body, as well as my observations after the body was found before your constables arrived, and a list of the guests."

He nodded. "I thought you might. If you would be good enough to share those it could be helpful."

I assured him that I would get him a report of my observations after I typed them out on the new *portable* typing machine that I had recently acquired and had installed at the office on the Strand.

It was much smaller than the enormous machine I usually used at the townhouse when creating my next novel, and was quite useful when writing reports on our inquiry cases.

It had been made available to me by a gentleman by the name of Laidlaw when we had met through my publisher Mr. Warren. Mr. Laidlaw's father had invented a portable typing machine. His son had attended university with James Warren and paid a visit when in London.

James, now married to my sister, had made our acquaintance at my last book signing.

That initial meeting included a conversation about my behemoth of a typing machine at the townhouse in Mayfair, and Mr. Laidlaw thought his portable machine might be of benefit.

When he returned to Glasgow, he arranged to ship one to me—an ingenious marketing ploy. It was quite marvelous, and I had it delivered to the office on the Strand.

I thought Brodie might have apoplexy when he discovered the cost of the machine. He was, after all, a Scot, and they are known for their thriftiness. The subject of finances was something that reared its head every once in a while.

Also characteristic of being a Scot, Brodie felt it was his responsibility to support me. I had been supporting myself with my writing for several years, and then there was a substantial inheritance for both my sister and me after our mother's death. I was quite independent in that regard.

"I will not have people thinkin' that I am living off yer title or yer inheritance. I can well take care of the both of us."

"Of course," I had replied at the time.

Therefore, we were still *discussing* that aspect of our marriage from time to time.

"Lady Forsythe, I believe?"

I turned and took in the appearance of a somewhat portly man, of an age somewhat older than Mr. Dooley, well dressed, and with an officious air about him.

"Yes," I replied.

I had not seen him among the guests earlier and concluded that he might either be with the museum or had arrived with Mr. Dooley.

"I am Inspector Todd with the Metropolitan Police."

That somewhat pretentious introduction answered the question.

"I understand that you were the last person to speak with Sir Nelson Lawrence."

"You are mistaken," I informed him. "I had gone to his office upon my arrival this morning, however he was not there. I then returned to the area outside the Egyptian room."

"That was before the exhibit opened," he concluded.

How very observant of him.

"Yes," I replied.

Brodie and Mr. Dooley had now returned.

"Is there some difficulty, Mr. Todd?" Mr. Dooley inquired.

"I was questioning Lady Forsythe on her whereabouts prior to the opening of the exhibit when the body was found," he replied. "She was seen leaving his office beforehand."

Mr. Dooley introduced Inspector Todd. I did discern a certain look that passed between Brodie and the man. Some difficulty perhaps on the part of both men.

"Sir Nelson was an acquaintance from my earlier travels," I explained. "I went to his office to congratulate him on his return to London and the exhibit."

"How well were you acquainted?" Inspector Todd inquired.

That seemed irrelevant, as there were several present who had also been personally acquainted with him, including my great aunt.

"I believe Lady Forsythe has already answered that question," Brodie informed him.

"Yes, however ..." He was obviously about to ask another question, but was cut off.

"Ye have her statement," Brodie sharply informed him. "I would suggest that ye get on with speaking to others here as well."

"If you recall, Mr. Brodie, it is our responsibility to question all parties concerned, no matter their station or title," he replied.

"And ye have done that ..."

Whatever the history was between the two men, I thought it best to diffuse the situation before there was further confrontation.

"I will be happy to provide a written statement in the matter," I informed Inspector Todd. "As well as one from my great aunt, Lady Montgomery."

"That will be sufficient," Mr. Dooley replied, then, "Best get on with yer duties, Mr. Todd."

As he departed, I thought of the saying 'If looks could kill.'

"The man has not changed," Brodie commented after he had gone.

"Only worse now," Mr. Dooley replied. "He was certain to take the interim position upon Abberline's suspension. It has not set well with him that the position was given to Chief Inspector Graham."

"That must make things difficult," I commented. It explained a great deal.

"That would be putting it lightly," Mr. Dooley replied. "Most of the other inspectors and constables make an effort to stay out of his way. Unfortunately, due to the number of guests here today and the fact that most of the other inspectors are off on other matters, he was sent along to assist. I apologize," he told us both.

"The man has not changed," Brodie remarked.

"Only more so," Dooley replied.

I excused myself then. I needed to find my great aunt. In spite of the fact that I had assured both Mr. Todd and Mr. Dooley that I would provide a statement from both my great aunt and myself, I was concerned should Inspector Todd insist on questioning her repeatedly, as he had me. I thought of her walking cane.

She was, after all, a descendant of William the Conqueror, who historically had ravaged England, and established himself as king, undoubtedly with a few hundred bodies strewn along the way. I had visions of a second badly bloodied corpse if Mr. Todd should persist.

The exhibit was subsequently closed until a full investigation could be completed.

Inspector Todd survived the day; however, he was most persistent that I provide a written statement for the investigation as soon as possible.

I learned from Mr. Dooley that Inspector Todd had attempted to speak with Mr. Hosni, Sir Nelson's assistant; however, there seemed to be some sort of a language barrier that prevented it. That seemed strange, since I had observed that Mr. Hosni spoke perfect English, but I could not fault the man for his reluctance to do so, given my encounter with Inspector Todd.

Afterward, once Mr. Dooley and his constables had collected evidence along with a list of names of those in attendance, the other guests were allowed to leave. Mr. Munro arrived to escorted my great aunt back to Sussex Square, while Brodie and I remained.

With substantial experience in such things and at the request of Mr. Dooley, he made his own observations of the murder scene. He used his pen to lift the edge of Sir Nelson's shirt away from the location of the wound.

He then checked for what he referred to as *other superficial wounds* on Sir Nelson's hands and fingers, as if there might have been a struggle. He stood, a thoughtful expression at his face.

"Wait here."

I watched as he discussed something with Mr. Dooley.

There was a nod of acknowledgement, then Brodie returned. He slipped his hand around my arm as Mr. Todd approached once more.

"You will deliver your statement to the Yard, Lady Forsythe," he reminded me.

It was not a request.

"Of course."

There was no usual parting comment as Brodie escorted me to the entrance to the exhibit room, where we were joined by Aunt Antonia.

"That man is quite full of himself," she commented, with a glare across the room at Inspector Todd.

"My deepest sympathy, Mr. Brodie, that you once worked with him. He does seem to have a very high opinion of himself. Such a vile creature."

I couldn't have said it better.

We then left the exhibit hall, where we found Munro waiting to escort my great aunt to her coach. She laid a hand on my arm.

"You must see this dreadful business resolved, my dear."

I assured her that we would, although with no assurance that we would be allowed to participate in the investigation with Mr. Todd on the case.

When she and Munro had departed, I caught sight of a figure standing a short distance apart, presently being questioned by one of the police constables. It was Mr. Hosni.

As I approached, the constable put away his notepad, apparently his questions concluded, then nodded in my direction as he departed to return to the exhibit hall.

"I tried to explain, Lady Forsythe," Hosni said, his expression quite distraught. "It is the curse. I warned Sir Nelson before we left Cairo. I could tell the constable thought it had nothing to do with this."

"What curse?" From my travels to Egypt, I was not unfamiliar with the reality that many believed in ancient curses. There had even been some discussion about it in my first trip there, where I encountered Sir Nelson Lawrence.

"I wanted to give him this amulet for protection," Mr. Hosni continued. He handed me the embossed gold medallion on a chain. I immediately recognized the figure embossed there.

It was the Eye of Horus, a familiar figure used for protection as I had learned in my travels to Egypt.

"He refused to carry it with him. He said that it was only superstition, that if there was any danger to him, it would have happened long ago when he first began his explorations."

That dark gaze bored into me. "He was a good man. He wanted only for others to understand my culture. It was not about taking these things from us. You will find who has done this?"

"I don't know if we will be allowed. The police seem to be in charge of this ..."

Before I could finish, his hand closed around mine.

"You will keep the amulet now. It will protect you."

Mr. Hosni bowed his head, then turned back to the office he had once shared with Sir Nelson. I couldn't help but wonder what would become of him now.

I would speak with the director of the museum. Perhaps a position as curator of the Egyptian exhibits. He was, after all, highly educated, as well as having been born and raised in Egypt.

Or perhaps he would choose to return to Cairo and work with the Ministry of Antiquities there.

"A curious man, Sir Nelson's assistant," Brodie commented. "What have ye there?"

He had managed to find a driver in spite of the throng of others who departed.

We climbed aboard and the driver slowly moved through the congestion of carriages and coaches, those who had been present when the exhibit opened gossiping among themselves. No doubt over the event of the morning.

"It's an amulet for protection, the Eye of Horus," I explained. "Mr. Hosni had tried to give it to Sir Nelson, but he insisted he didn't need it."

"And now he's given it to ye?"

"Supposedly there is some sort of curse attached to the statue of Ramses II. He said the amulet would protect me."

"A curse. I suppose that would be much like a *geas*," he commented in Gaelic.

I was familiar with some Gaelic words from spending time at Old Lodge, my great aunt's residence in Scotland, where I had spent weeks at a time exploring the forest and glens surrounding the old hunting lodge. And then there were the words I had learned from Brodie.

"There was an old woman in Edinburgh who sold apples when we were lads livin' on the streets," he explained. "When we had nothin' to eat, we might pinch an apple or two from her. She would curse us for it. It has to do with spirits and such, like the kelpies and ancient monsters in the lochs."

An old woman who heaped curses on young boys. Still, there was no anger or regret in Brodie's voice. Just a story of a boy on his own, as I knew he had been.

"Ye believe in such things?" he asked.

"I don't *disbelieve*," I replied. "I've seen many things in my travels that have no other explanation.

"Mr. Hosni asked that we find the person who killed Sir Nelson. Although it would seem that Mr. Todd is certainly determined to handle the matter himself," I added.

"Ye want us to make our own inquiries."

"Sir Nelson was a friend," I replied. "He took it upon himself to assist a naïve and somewhat reckless person, and others, in understanding the Egyptian culture and history. He was a very kind man and devoted to the people there.

"Aye, naïve and reckless," he commented with a slightly bemused expression.

I chose to ignore it.

"I feel a responsibility to help. It could be simply a matter of a robbery gone terribly wrong, or it might be something else. There were a great many valuable artifacts in the exhibit. The director of the museum will be able to determine if anything is missing."

"Aye," Brodie replied. "I've already spoken with Mr. Dooley in the matter. He will welcome anything we might be able to add to the investigation. He will have a word with Mr. Graham, the acting Chief Inspector, so there is no difficulty with Mr. Todd."

That was, of course, more easily said than done.

Three

LATE AFTERNOON, we received word from Mr. Dooley that Sir Nelson's body had been taken to a holding room at the Old Scotland Yard for further inspection by the police surgeon before being released. A nephew, the son of Sir Nelson's sister, had been contacted regarding the explorer's death.

Mr. Brimley, a chemist with a shop in the East End and good friend in past inquiry cases, was not available at the moment, but promised to meet us at the Yard. His expertise was always welcome as he had a great deal of experience with a variety of wounds—both accidental and otherwise.

He was also a good friend who had provided care and assistance when it was most needed, including a bullet wound I had sustained in the pursuit of a past case.

Brodie had been most circumspect during our ride to the office on the Strand and afterward, as I made my preliminary notes about our observations in the matter of Sir Nelson's murder on the chalkboard. It was obvious there was something turning over in his thoughts that he chose, for the time being, not to discuss.

I was accustomed to his ruminations when on an inquiry case. It usually came from some prior experience in his time with the Metropolitan Police, some case he had worked, or even a case that we had worked together.

I now stepped back from the board and circled back to the additional desk that currently occupied the office of the Strand, a piece my great aunt had delivered and insisted that I use, with a comment that it had once belonged to some distant ancestor or another ... she couldn't remember.

"It is only gathering dust tucked away upstairs. You might as well have the use of it," she had explained.

It was quite old in the style I had seen in the rectory of any old church. It was no use to point out that it might have historical importance. Once Aunt Antonia had decided on a matter, that was the end of it.

It was quite lovely and had been cared for before being stored away in the Normandy room, as she called it—a reference to our common ancestor William of Normandy.

The room also contained an a very old, long table that smelled of very old oak, with several notable gouges in it near the head of the table.

"He was rumored to always carry a knife," she had once told me when I was exploring the room at Sussex Square that had been built about the same time as William's rule as King of England.

"And he had a fiery temper according to family archives. I suppose he might have used the knife to make his point during a conversation or argument."

Discovering various ancestors had been a favorite pastime. And we had a great many of them.

"All of this," she had continued, *"will go to you and your sister when I am gone. Except for the Viking longboat."*

That was a story for another day. I will concede that for some, my great aunt had been considered to be somewhat eccentric. As for myself, I adored her.

She was an example of a woman who had chosen to live her life exactly as she pleased and didn't give a fig what anyone thought.

Except that is, when it came to Brodie. As I had discovered since that first inquiry case regarding my sister's disappearance.

"You will contact him," she had told me at the time, when the MET seemed unconcerned in the matter and had treated it as nothing more than a disaffected wife who had taken herself off.

"He can be trusted, refuses to back down when a situation becomes difficult, and will see the matter done," she had added most emphatically, which raised the question for me at the time, just how had she made the acquaintance of a private inquiry man?

It was only later I discovered the answer, when there was a far different conversation regarding other aspects about Brodie. The sort of conversation one does not usually expect to have with a woman of her station or one who was eighty-four years old at the time.

"There is a great deal to be said for a man who can make your toes curl."

Indeed!

"I could be tempted, even at my age," she had added.

No comment to that!

However, as I discovered, Brodie was very much a man of strong character. He could be quite stubborn from time to time, but much like Rupert the hound—certainly not a criticism—he refused to walk away from a difficult situation.

He was quite handsome in a scowling sort of way, with

dark hair that seemed to constantly be in need of a trim, dark beard, and that penetrating dark gaze that had a way of looking at me in a way that suggested far more.

And then there was that toe-curling part of it that my great aunt had spoken of.

We had our ups and downs, as my sister had once observed. We disagreed on things from time to time, but I respected where he had come from, and the heart-breaking aspects of his childhood.

What was a woman who had traveled, experienced many adventures, and taken risks, to do with all of that?

I would take it, an adventure to be certain.

I returned to my desk, inserted paper into the typewriter, and began typing my statement for Mr. Dooley regarding the discovery of Sir Nelson's body by my great aunt. Along with a statement regarding my brief visit to Sir Nelson's office and my conversation with Mr. Hosni.

As arranged with Mr. Dooley, we arrived late afternoon at the building adjacent to the New Scotland Yard, on the Victoria Embankment. This location served as additional administrative offices and included a morgue where bodies were taken in the course of investigations.

The New Scotland Yard also retained the services of their own surgeon, who added his examination to police reports. We had encountered the surgeon on previous investigations. He seemed competent in most instances, yet we also relied on Mr. Brimley's observations as well.

Mr. Brimley had been educated at King's College, and devoted his services to the poor in the East End with his chemist shop in Holborn. He was also a scientist. That was the best way to describe his experiments and study of body parts, mostly hands or other appendages, due to an accident.

He collected specimens and put them in jars with formaldehyde so that he could study them. He had also been known to dissect a specimen in his own investigations of how the human body worked. I often found him examining some piece of tissue under a microscope in the back of his shop.

Mr. Brimley joined us now, somewhat distracted over a situation he had been ministering to when Brodie requested his assistance.

"Poor girl got caught up in a family way," he explained. "A young actress. Went to one of the women who assist with those situations. Dreadful business that. Your friend, Templeton, brought her to me. She'd lost a great deal of blood afterward, and very nearly her life.

"She'll recover, poor thing. But most likely never be able to have a family of her own." He looked up, somewhat myopically behind the glasses he usually wore.

"Now what is the business about a body found at the museum?"

We entered through the main entrance of that adjacent building at the Embankment, and Brodie signed us in after informing the young constable that we were assisting Inspector Dooley in an investigation. He then made the request to see the body that had been taken there from the museum.

I have seen several bodies in the course of my travels and since that first inquiry case that Brodie and I shared in the disappearance of my sister.

There is always that initial surprise, even shock. It then gives way to the matter at hand, attempting to learn something about the victim and the person who committed the crime.

Brodie is convinced there is something wrong with me in

that regard, as I am not given to fainting at such things, although there was the body I saw before, when on one of my adventures.

The poor man had been the victim of some difficulty and was found floating in the Nile as we reached shore at one of the many small ports along the river. He had been there for some time and was covered with flies, his features bloated and distorted.

Not a great experience. Yet it prepared me for the bodies of victims Brodie and I encountered in our inquiry cases. As he once told me, after I insisted that I would not be set aside in such things, it was best to concentrate on the clues that might be found that would help us find who had committed the murder.

We were escorted by another constable to the 'holding room' where Sir Nelson's body had been taken. It was here that the police surgeon would perform his examination of bodies and make his reports that would become part of the police reports.

The room was sterile, with a dozen tables, half of them draped with sheets that might be found in a hospital. Along one wall was a line of eight cabinets where bodies were placed on ice, if needed, before an examination could be performed.

Not a pleasant thought, being put on ice and then into a drawer. According to Mr. Brimley, it preserved the body for a certain amount of time until arrangements could be made by family, or ... very often in matters that involved the MET, the deceased person remained anonymous, and was buried in an unnamed grave.

I did have a somewhat philosophical view of such things. Once a person was gone, they were gone. My friend Templeton, however, who is quite famous as an actress, had a far different view. She was absolutely certain that some form of the human spirit continued on *after*.

She had dabbled a bit in spiritualism, and claimed to have a connection with Sir William Shakespeare, who had been dead for well over two centuries. He supposedly had a habit of popping in from time to time with advice, an opinion, or in a tirade depending on the situation.

I didn't argue the point with her. In fact, I had to admit that she had provided information, supposedly received from Sir William, that had provided an important clue in our inquiry cases.

Who was I to argue?

Brodie and Mr. Brimley gathered round the examination table where Sir Nelson had been laid out. The sheet was drawn back as the constable in charge informed us that the surgeon had not yet made his observations.

I assumed my pragmatic manner and joined them as Mr. Brimley adjusted his glasses and leaned in close for his own observations. There was the usual mumbling, speaking more to himself, as he reached for an instrument from the steel table nearby.

He proceeded to probe the wound in Sir Nelson's chest with more mumbled comments as he described his findings, while Brodie was intent on his own observations in that way of a former police inspector.

As for myself, I took out my notebook and made notes as I followed Mr. Brimley around the table, as I did when he was asked to assist us. I was not prepared when he abruptly pulled back the sheet, much like a magician, and revealed that Sir Nelson was completely naked.

"Oh."

At least I was fairly certain that was my reaction, as I was not accustomed to seeing a naked man, with one exception, of course. And most certainly not one fully displayed like a fish laid out at market, right down to …

"Apologies, miss," Mr. Brimley said.

I immediately averted my gaze and concentrated on my notes, even as I heard Brodie clear his throat.

Or was that laughter? I refused to look at him.

"Are ye all right, lass?"

"Quite all right," I assured him, still refusing to look at him. Knowing Brodie, he would not let the moment go without later comment.

"What conclusions would you draw, Mr. Brimley?" I asked the chemist in order to move the situation along.

"Knife wound for certain," he commented. "The edges are clean cut and deep. From the angle and position of the wound, it was made by someone of even height and very obviously pierced the heart. There would have been a great deal of blood," he recited quite methodically.

"Death would have been almost immediate," he continued. "The heart is usually the last organ to die; however, with a direct wound it would have been very quick indeed. And with the *rigor mortis* that I'm seeing …" He poked the lower leg, then attempted to flex it.

"Death was approximately eight to ten hours ago."

That would mean that Sir Nelson's body had lain in the exhibit hall for a good deal of time before my great aunt discovered it.

"There is no external bruising as if there might have been a struggle. That would suggest that he was most likely come upon quite suddenly. I would guess that under the circumstances you've explained—the locked exhibit room, the last time his assistant saw him, that he might very well have known his attacker."

"What about a particular scent about the body?" Brodie inquired.

Scent? Was that the thoughtful look I saw on his face as he bent over Sir Nelson's corpse? Something he sensed at the scene of the murder?

"There is a certain scent," Mr. Brimley replied with a furrowed brow. "I'm not familiar with it, though. My guess would be that it's not alcohol nor narcotics. Both have a familiar smell to them."

I tucked my notebook under my arm and rounded the table. Mr. Brimley had pulled the sheet back up over the body. The scent was faint at first, then slightly stronger as I leaned closer. I immediately recognized it.

It was quite refreshing, for all that it was on a very dead body, a subtle blend of herbs, perhaps rosemary with an undertone of spice.

"It's absinthe," I said with some surprise, and not at all something I would have expected, as the man I had known was very simple in his dress and manner, with no time for such things as he was always off and about on some archeological site.

Even his manner of dress that morning had obviously been somewhat hasty, more concerned about the opening of the exhibit than proper dress etiquette or formalities. With shirt sleeves rolled back, he'd had a slightly disheveled appearance that was quite familiar, even under the circumstances.

Once we'd completed our examinations, Mr. Brimley was eager to get back to his 'patient,' as he referred to the young woman he had attended. He kept a small room at the back of his shop for those who might be injured and need his assistance. I had spent a night there after a particularly difficult inquiry case when I was injured.

We departed as well. I had my notes of his observations as well as our own. I left an envelope for Mr. Dooley that contained my statement about the events of the morning and asked that the constable on duty see that he received it.

Now, as the coach pulled away from the front entrance of the New Scotland Yard building that sprawled along the embankment, I felt that dark gaze watching me.

"Are ye all right?" Brodie gently inquired.

In spite of his amusement at my reaction to seeing Sir Nelson, naked as the day he was born, I heard the concern in his voice.

"He was a friend. I know it canna be easy."

He did know, with far too much experience in the matter of brutal murders, including his own mother years before, in his work with the MET, and now with our inquiry cases.

"He made my travel to Egypt exciting and so very interesting," I replied. "Not at all pretentious or bothered by dozens of questions, or put off by a woman, as others were," I replied, recalling that first adventure to that part of the world.

"He was much like a kindly uncle, eager to show me his latest exploration site, filled with such excitement. This exhibit was very special to him. He was so eager to share it with everyone."

Brodie leaned across the coach and took my hand. "And ye feel a responsibility to find who did this."

I nodded. "It's the least that I can do."

"Tell me about absinthe," he said as the coach lurched through early evening traffic across London.

"It's a fairly common fragrance. Templeton wears it. She

insists that it heightens her sensitivity to messages from the spirit world."

"Ah, Sir William Shakespeare," he replied.

I heard the skepticism.

"He has provided information in the past," I pointed out.

"That might have been a lucky guess on Templeton's part," he pointed out as he sat back.

"Not at all," I defended my friend. "She was most accurate and the information was helpful."

"And now a man wearing a woman's perfume?" he commented.

"It's not merely a woman's perfume," I pointed out. "Men wear it as well, usually in a pomade," though certainly not the man sitting across from me with that mane of overlong dark hair.

"Or for other personal ... reasons."

That dark gaze met mine. "Personal reasons?"

He had taken to using my bathing soap, a clear, amber bar, simply because it was 'there,' as he said.

I was quite partial to that faintly spicy scent of green things that reminded me of the forest near Old Lodge in the north. He seemed to like it as well.

"From what ye've told me of the man, he did not seem the 'fashionable' sort."

I agreed. "Not at all."

Which brought me back round to my first thought, that it was very possible that the smell of absinthe had possibly been worn by his murderer?

We arrived back at the office on the Strand to find a message from Inspector Dooley. It was brief and most urgent.

Howard Carter, Sir Nelson's young assistant, had been

taken to the Bow Street station for questioning in the matter of Sir Nelson's death, and then arrested!

"I refuse to believe that he had anything to do with it!" I vehemently replied.

"In spite of that," Brodie pointed out, "he has been arrested. According to this, he will be remanded to the Bow Street criminal court in the morning, where formal charges will be read against him."

I was fairly certain I saw Inspector Todd's hand in this— the murder of a member of a prominent old London family, a room full of possible suspects, many of whom were very influential people, and a police inspector most eager to make a name for himself, no matter if the person was guilty, or not.

"I want to see Howard Carter."

"I thought ye might. I will see if Mr. Dooley can make the necessary arrangement."

Brodie was eventually able to speak with Mr. Dooley, and learned that he had encountered some difficulty with Inspector Todd.

He had attempted to take the matter directly to the Interim Chief Inspector, Mr. Graham, but wasn't able to speak with him. It would have to wait until morning.

It seemed that young Mr. Carter would have to spend the night in a holding cell at the Bow Street police station.

"There is nothing to be done before morning," Brodie said as the telephone call ended.

"We'll go first thing. If necessary, I'll speak with the Chief Inspector myself. Perhaps we can buy more time to find the one who killed Sir Nelson."

It was not what I wanted, but it would have to do. I knew only too well the often difficult and cumbersome workings of the Metropolitan Police.

"I know wot yer thinkin'," Brodie told me. "But it will do no good to worry the matter. Ye need supper. Bring yer notes and we'll see what there is there that might be useful."

Four

WE STAYED at the Strand that night. I hardly slept, then finally gave up and discovered that Brodie was already up and about in the adjacent office.

It was barely light beneath the edge of the new window shades my great aunt had installed after declaring that we could hardly stay over with people able to peer in the windows at night.

I didn't bother to remind her that the office and the adjacent room were on the second floor and unless a person was an acrobat capable of scaling buildings or proficient with stilts, we were hardly at risk of being 'seen,' as she put it.

Brodie had the coffee steaming on the coal stove, and presently sat at the desk going over the notes that I had made the day before. He looked up as I came out into the outer office.

His hair was slightly mussed from that habit of pushing his hand back through the thick waves when he was distracted or deep in thought, and the dark beard shadowed his face.

I had discovered that I did like mornings when the day had not yet begun and it was just the two of us, though I had always been most efficient on my own. My sister was certain there was something wrong with me.

"Don't you ever get lonely at the townhouse with only Mrs. Ryan and then off on your adventures where you don't know another soul? I shouldn't want to spend my life all alone."

I had never considered myself *lonely*. I wasn't bothered by the usual trappings of society. I occasionally participated in one of my great aunt's celebrations, but other than that, I was quite content to not have my life dictated to by the needs of another.

Deep down I did know where it came from. Our childhood had not been easy after the loss of both our parents.

Our mother had died and our father shortly thereafter by his own hand, leaving us to somehow survive the wreckage he had made of our lives. As a result, I learned very early not to trust anyone but myself. And at the age of nine years, I was determined to take care of my sister and myself.

Slightly misguided, since we had no home, very little money except for an inheritance from our mother, which our father had decimated quite thoroughly with his gambling debts.

The truth was that I didn't trust anyone, after watching the debt collectors invade our home with their lists, as they calculated how much might be made from the sale of everything to pay the remaining debts, which were substantial.

If not for our great aunt, my sister and I would have been cast out onto the street. Much like Brodie.

In spite of the obvious differences in our stations, we had that in common. And other things as well.

But most of all, I could trust him. Not that it had come easily. It had unfortunately taken that first inquiry case together, my sister's life in danger, and my great aunt's insistence that he was the only person who could help us—a man I could trust.

He sat at the desk now, going over my notes. Slightly distracted, he glanced up at the chalkboard, where it had become a habit to write out the clues we discovered in a case, along with names of suspects.

I had erased the board after our previous inquiry case; however, he had obviously made notes there after our encounter at the museum and the murder of Sir Nelson the day before.

Who said that you couldn't teach an old dog new tricks?

Not that he was old, or a dog. Most certainly not, as I took in that distracted countenance, and most particularly that slightly disheveled dark hair and the faint line between the slash of dark brows—the thin line of a scar through the one on the left from a previous confrontation in one of our cases.

It did give him a stirring appearance, most particularly with the collar of his shirt undone.

I poured myself a cup of coffee and sat in the chair across from the desk and studied the board.

He had made a notation regarding Mr. Hosni, simply written as *Sir Nelson's assistant*.

As for our observations of the situation, he had listed several—where the body was found, the position of the body, the weapon used, that there were no apparent signs of a struggle, and that curious scent.

"I should like to speak to the director of the museum to learn if anything was missing from the exhibit," I commented. "Although it is possible the police have already done so, Mr. Todd being quite *efficient*."

That was one word to describe the man. I thought of another—arrogant.

"He was most condescending, full of himself, annoying, not to mention patronizing. I can only think that he is undoubtedly not married. What woman would put up with such a man?"

Actually, that was several words when one would do—contemptuous.

"Certainly not one such as yerself." That dark gaze met mine.

"Wot do ye *really* think of the man?" he asked.

"I will undoubtedly be able to come up with more. He is most deplorable." I continued to stare at the board.

"I would also like to find out more about Sir Nelson's nephew. Mr. Dooley mentioned that the body would be released to him. He might be able to provide some insight, if Sir Nelson had any recent confrontations with anyone, although I cannot imagine it.

"Aunt Antonia seemed to be somewhat acquainted with the family. She might be able to provide something there," I added.

"Aye, and it might be useful to speak with Mr. Brown, regarding any rumors of stolen or smuggled artifacts."

I was uneasy about that. The man was a dangerous sort. He had provided important information in the past—a favor he called it, and expected a favor from Brodie in return.

It was one of those arrangements with people who acquired information on the streets, and it could be dangerous. I caught the look Brodie gave me.

"What are ye thinkin?"

"The man is dangerous."

"Aye, that he is. We have a mutual respect in that regard."

"And you owe *him* a favor," I pointed out.

"Are ye worried about me?"

That dark gaze softened with amusement. He could be such a devil at times.

"You have not specified what arrangements you might want in the event you suffered some dreadful encounter with the man."

"Arrangements?"

The amusement was still there.

"I've not given it much thought," he replied. "I dinna fancy a Viking longboat like yerself or her ladyship, nor any weeping nor wailing."

"I am not the weeping or wailing sort."

"I've noticed."

"With a man like Mr. Brown, you might want to consider it," I replied. "I do not appreciate the thought of being awakened by Mr. Dooley or Mr. Cavendish to inform me that you've been found in some alleyway, or not found at all. And there is that favor. Mr. Brown might decide to collect."

"He is not a fool," Brodie commented. "Not when someone is of value to him for information as well. And ye needn't worry on that account. I have more than repaid the favor. He is now the one who owes me."

"When did this occur?" I remarked with more than a little surprise.

There had been no mention of it. Still, in spite of the fact that we worked together and there was now our personal relationship, there were frequent occasions when he was out and about the city on some matter or another, and I had no idea where he might have gone.

"Ye dinna want to know, lass. The *when* and the *how* doesna matter. It is done and the man is now indebted to me. I know where he can be found and I will put out the word to meet."

That did not reassure me about his association with Mr. Brown.

"And ye are correct about the possibility of stolen artifacts. I will make inquiries in that regard. What about the assistant, Mr. Hosni? He might be motivated to steal a valuable piece or two."

That was a possibility not to be overlooked.

"It would have been easy enough for him," Brodie pointed out. "He had access to both the exhibit and Sir Nelson."

No stone unturned. It did seem as if we had several stones, as it were.

"I will see him when I return to the museum, although I find it difficult to believe that he would have anything to do with Sir Nelson's murder. He has been with him for several years, and undoubtedly had many opportunities, if he was so inclined."

"Perhaps. But there is the possibility that Sir Nelson only recently discovered that some pieces were missing and confronted the man," Brodie added. "And be mindful of that curse."

"Do you believe in them after all?" I was somewhat surprised at that.

"There are those that believe such things and carry out some practices against evil spirits. I wouldna want ye to cross paths with such. I've come to like ye the way ye are, and dinna fancy ye turned into some vile creature."

There was suddenly a sound at the landing, the bell ringing to announce that someone had arrived.

He went out onto the landing, then returned.

"Mr. Dooley," he announced as he pulled me up out of the chair.

"Although I verra much admire ye in yer shift, I dinna want

him to see ye in such a way." He drew me against him, brushed my hair back from my cheek, and kissed me. "I dinna share what is mine."

I should have been put off by what some might have considered to be such an old-fashioned notion. After all, I considered myself to be a modern woman.

I wasn't put off and kissed him back. I knew where it came from, and, oddly, it meant far more to me than anything, that he had let me into his life, into that painful history ... into his heart. Even if he was not one to admit such things.

"Go now. Put on yer clothes, before I send Mr. Dooley on his way and bolt the door."

And there was that also. Tempting as it was, I returned to the bedroom, dressed, and joined Brodie and Mr. Dooley in the outer office.

"There's word about the investigation into the matter of Sir Nelson's murder," Brodie informed me as I poured us both another cup of coffee and handed one to him.

"I thought it best to come here since you have a particular interest in the case," Mr. Dooley explained. "Rather than discuss the matter by way of the telephone." He gave Brodie a meaningful look.

"The walls have ears."

Ears that might get word to Inspector Todd? Not the first time I had heard that in regard to the Metropolitan Police, a veritable nest of rumor and gossip for an institution that should not have condoned either.

"The family was contacted about the death, more specifically Sir Nelson's nephew," he continued. "It seems there is a bit of an estrangement there."

"What sort of estrangement?" I inquired.

"We were not provided an explanation, only informed that there is no interest in providing for the body," he replied.

That was a most surprising development. I could not imagine experiencing a death in the family and not wanting to provide burial or some other means of sending him off.

Well, actually I could, speaking from my own family experience.

However, Sir Nelson was highly respected and most certainly his family was very proud of his accomplishments.

Or, apparently not.

There had been no further explanation, yet it raised several questions, the main one being, what sort of estrangement?

Brodie thanked him for bringing us the information.

"It might well be that anything you are able to learn could be important to the investigation," Mr. Dooley added.

"What about Inspector Todd?" I inquired. "Surely he will be pursuing his own inquiries."

"You did not hear it from me, but he is pursuing robbery as the motive."

"And ye are not so certain that is the reason for the crime," Brodie concluded.

"There were a great many valuable artifacts that were part of the exhibit that could have easily been taken as well but were not, including the murder weapon."

Speaking of that ...

"Might it be possible to more closely inspect the dagger?" I asked.

"Ye have a particular reason?" Brodie commented.

"In my travels I have learned that there are often specific meanings with such things—carvings, etchings, symbols, that sort of thing. It might be able to tell us something."

Mr. Dooley nodded. "I'll arrange for ye to inspect it, in

confidence mind you. It would have to be when Mr. Todd is out and about on another matter. The dagger is currently in the evidence room at Bow Street."

"That could be useful," Brodie agreed.

"I'll see what can be arranged," Mr. Dooley replied. "Perhaps a special request for Mr. Todd in another matter that would take him into another part of the city for several hours." He rose from the chair across the desk.

"And I thought Mr. Abberline was a horse's arse. He was obvious when he meddled with things, but this one," he shook his head. "He's sneaky, going about behind one's back, always looking to trip one up and make himself look important."

Sneaky, an interesting word.

"You might want to be careful, Miss Forsythe," Mr. Dooley added. "He has a particular dislike for those better than him, which is most others."

As he turned to leave, I did inquire if he had received my written statement about my observations at the museum the previous day.

"When might you have delivered it?"

I explained that I had given it to one of the constables at the Bow Street Station. However, with his question, it did seem that it might have been 'delayed' somehow.

"I'll inquire about it. It might have been lost along the way and necessary for you to write it up once again and have it delivered directly to me."

It did seem as if it might have landed on some other desk.

"What is it about the MET that inspires such inefficiency?" I asked Brodie, when Dooley had gone after providing the address where Sir Nelson's nephew lived with his wife.

"The pay is not wot it should be for the responsibilities a

man is asked to take on, even for inspectors," he replied. Certainly, the voice of experience.

"And there are the temptations on the streets—protection money paid by merchants that might mean an officer's release or even imprisonment if it was known, and other opportunities that come their way."

"Prostitution?" I was not naïve to such things.

"Aye, and some kind of payment received to look the other way in certain situations."

I didn't ask the obvious question. In consideration of his past, it was obvious that he was familiar with such things.

"It could be useful for me to speak with Aunt Antonia about the estrangement in Sir Nelson's family that Mr. Dooley spoke of," I replied. "She might know something about it, or in the least have heard something. Gossip being what it is."

A veritable information network, I thought, and often quite reliable. And my great aunt was usually well informed about such things.

I placed a telephone call to Sussex Square to inquire if she was about. One never knew, with a variety of social engagements or perhaps out and about in her motor carriage. If she had nothing else on her engagement calendar, she had been known to take herself off, 'practicing her driving skills about the city,' as she explained it.

No one in London was safe; however, I would never have said that to her. I had simply put both Lily and Mr. Munro on notice that she was to be accompanied at all times.

I had visions of her ending up in some dangerous part of the city. Not that I was necessarily afraid for her, but concerned for whomever she encountered armed with her walking stick and I suspected some additional weapon that she had retrieved from the Sword Room at Sussex Square.

I supposed there was something to be said for someone her age who had seen and lived a great deal and was quite fearless when it came to such things. Let those unfortunate ones who encountered her in such circumstances be forewarned.

It was a warm spring day, for London, the gardens that lined the carriage way from the front gate at Sussex Square already in bloom.

Aunt Antonia was not out and about in London, but out and about in the gardens and the green beyond the manor, I was informed.

Mr. Symons, her head butler, greeted me at the front entrance when I arrived.

"So very glad you are here now, Miss Mikaela," he said with definite uneasiness before I could even announce my arrival with the bell pull.

"Has something happened?" I inquired at his tone.

"Over forty years, miss."

"I beg your pardon?"

"The number of years I have been in service to her Ladyship. In that time, I have seen a great many things and never once complained. Perhaps a suggestion or two."

Something had most definitely happened.

"What is it? Has something happened to my aunt, or Lily?" I replied with growing concern.

Lily, the young girl who was now my ward, seemed to have recovered quite well from her involvement in our last inquiry case. Yet I worried about her. Certainly not over any physical injury except a few scrapes and bruises. It was her manner, definitely changed by the circumstances of the case. She had been most serious ever since.

"Miss Lily is quite well. She is in the upstairs library at her studies, with her tutor to arrive shortly."

Any further explanation was suddenly interrupted by a loud crash and the distinct sound of shattering glass.

"Good heavens!"

"Most certainly, miss."

My first thought was that my great aunt might have driven the motor carriage into the rear of the manor, although she had seemed to be quite accomplished the last I saw, aside from terrorizing people and horses on the Strand when she paid a surprise visit.

Surprise indeed.

At yet another explosion, servants scattered from various rooms in the back of the manor as if under fire on a battlefield.

"On the green near the motor track, the last anyone dared to observe," Mr. Symons informed me.

"More driving lessons?" I inquired.

"Not precisely, miss."

I handed him my umbrella and bag, and turned down the long hallway that led past the great hall, the formal parlor, and the garden room.

"Do be careful, miss," he cautioned.

Sussex Square was one of the few remaining original fortress residences still standing over the past several hundred years, built by my great ancestor, William the Conqueror, for his wife.

According to my great aunt, when the lady refused to join him from Normandy, he had instead installed his mistress of the moment.

When in Britain, ravaging, pillaging, and so on ... It was a rather colorful family history.

Over the centuries the original fortress had been expanded, added to, and remodeled, in a combination of Medieval, Tudor, and Georgian architecture that still included the original medieval wall built around the estate for protection.

The only thing missing was a tower that had apparently been taken down by another ancestor a couple of centuries earlier. I would have liked to explore the old tower with crenellations for pouring boiling oil on those below, and arrow slits for archers to fire on invaders beyond the wall.

There was another loud crash as I passed the great hall, the kitchens, servants' quarters, and stepped out onto the veranda, a later addition, that led to the gardens, the automobile track, and ...

An object that greatly resembled a golf ball took out another window overhead on the second floor. It was followed by my great aunt's *ballyhoo* in greeting.

"If you find it, please do pick it up," she called out as she approached. "I only have a dozen of them and I do not want to lose any."

Golf ball? I could only wonder when this had happened.

"The weather is quite marvelous," she continued, "at least one or two hours each day. I thought I would give it a go. I considered argyle socks, however, they might be too warm. What do you think?" She pirouetted in her latest costume.

The citizens of London had been spared the argyle socks. Not so the rest of her ensemble; that consisted of three-piece tweed golfing attire that included knickers, shirt and tie, stockings with short boots, leather gloves, and what could only be described as a jaunty cap set atop her hair that had been tucked under the brim.

Never let it be said that my great aunt didn't dress the part. And there was the golf club she carried.

"Most appropriate," I commented. "And it is a most formidable weapon."

I didn't bother to point out that her costume was what men usually wore when playing golf.

"I did notice some broken glass," I mentioned.

"My swing was a bit off," she conceded. "However, practice makes perfect and Munro did say that I was becoming quite proficient. Did you know that golf was banned for a time in Scotland for one reason or another?" She paused as we returned to the veranda.

"What brings you here, my dear? Is Brodie with you?"

"He's making inquiries regarding the situation at the museum yesterday."

"Oh, yes. Dreadful business that. Any idea who might have done such a dreadful thing?"

"We will be making some inquiries. That is the reason I'm here. You seem to be acquainted with Sir Nelson's family, and I thought you might be able to provide some insight that could be useful. Particularly as regards the nephew and Sir Nelson's sister."

Her face lit up. "Of course, in whatever way I might be of assistance," she replied, as we sat at the table on the veranda.

"Henry Sutcliffe was the father's name," my great aunt said over a glass of lemonade. "A bit of a ne'er-do-well. The sister ran off with him against their father's wishes.

"As I recall there was a bit of a dust-up over that, all sorts of rumors, and when they returned only a handful of months later, there was a child. Such folly to get caught like that." She took another sip of lemonade.

"That apparently did not go over well at all; however, their father was in failing health at that time, and young Nelson had taken himself off on his first expedition to Egypt."

Young Nelson. That did seem somewhat odd as he was considerably older than Brodie.

"He returned when the father died," my great aunt continued. "However, he was well into his travels and exploring about and had no interest in seeing to the family estate or any business interests.

"It was said that some financial arrangement was made for the sister, her husband, and young Sutcliffe as well, and then Sir Nelson took himself off to Egypt once again. That would have been around the time you made his acquaintance."

"Was there any difficulty with the financial arrangement that was made with his sister?"

"I don't recall … however, there is someone who might know. It seems that a lawyer of Sir Robert Laughton's acquaintance was to handle the arrangement, even though Sir Nelson had taken himself off by then. He might be able to assist with information in that regard."

I made a mental note to inquire with Sir Robert. He had been able to assist in other matters in the past regarding our inquiry cases.

"Are you and Brodie settling in at the Strand?"

"Yes, quite well when we stay over," I replied. "The bathroom is quite sufficient, and with a shower compartment."

"There are other furnishings here that might accommodate as well," she added. "We are a bit over-crowded with things acquired over the years. You might have a look."

It did seem unnecessary since we were not certain we would be remaining at the Strand. Brodie had yet to receive word from the new owner.

I assured my great aunt that we were quite comfortable.

"A cold box perhaps," she suggested. "One of those new electric ones. Cook says they are quite marvelous. We have four of them."

She was already up and back at it, making her way across the veranda, club in hand. I quickly made my way back inside, even as one of the groundskeepers swept up glass on the slate walkway.

The information my great aunt had provided was helpful. It might be useful to pay a visit to Sir Nelson's nephew.

Before leaving, I went to the upstairs library, where Lily was studying in preparation for a visit with her tutor later that morning.

Although recovered physically from the events in our previous inquiry case, Brodie and I had both noticed that change in her. Admittedly, the circumstances that had found her abducted and held prisoner by the murderer in that particular case would have been traumatic for anyone.

Yet, she was not some coddled innocent. She had experienced certain things surviving on her own in Edinburgh. I had seen that inner strength and resilience firsthand. For one so young, she reminded me much of myself.

Still, there was that change, something along with the resilience and strength. Something that was more introspective and quite serious, along with the occasional impudence and sass.

It did seem that the girl I had first encountered in another case and had taken as my ward, had become a young woman as a result of that recent experience.

She looked up as I entered the library. There was that familiar smile in greeting, but there was a different expression in her eyes.

We exchanged greetings, and I made the usual inquiries

about her progress. At the same time, I knew from updates from her tutor that she had a very keen mind and a quick grasp of everything she was learning.

"History?" I commented with a glance down at the enormous volume very much like the one I had once studied spread before her on the table.

"It is fascinating," she acknowledged, with a frown. "Did ye know that the Romans invaded England and stayed for over three hundred years until we threw them out?"

I acknowledged that I was aware of that, and we were off on a conversation about my travels, including my several-months-long first trip to Egypt that included time in Rome on the return.

She had heard, of course, about the new exhibit at the museum. I had planned to take her there once all the excitement of the new opening had worn off and the crowds were fewer. All of that was changed by the events of the day before.

"Will ye be taking the case to find the murderer?" she asked.

"We are making inquiries through people we know. An acquaintance of Brodie's asked that we find out what we could."

There was that thoughtful expression again. "What about the knife?"

It seemed that she had learned a great deal from my great aunt.

"It is presently with the Metropolitan Police as evidence of the crime."

"Is it always the same with a case? I mean, how you go about it, like ye did with the case about Miss Charlotte?"

She *was* in a very thoughtful mood this morning.

"There are usually clues at the beginning. As we follow

those clues, we frequently learn other information that can be helpful."

"Wot clues do ye have now?"

I went over the few things we did know, along with people who might be able to tell us more.

There was that somber expression again.

"Do ye have to be a certain age to be a private inquiry person?"

"It's not a matter of age, but of experience," I explained. "Brodie was with the MET for several years and he has a knowledge of the streets here in London. I don't have that same experience; still, I am acquainted with certain people who might be able to provide information on a matter. And I've learned a great deal along the way as well."

She was quite serious. "I've been thinkin'."

Five

I THOUGHT of what I was able to learn from my great aunt about Sir Nelson's family as I made the return trip to the museum to speak with the director and Mr. Hosni.

There had most definitely been family difficulties in the past with Sir Nelson. And still?

It would certainly explain his nephew's refusal to see to Sir Nelson's funeral arrangements.

From my great aunt I had also learned the Lawrence family manor house was gone, sold some time before, as the Lawrence estate was lost to mounting debts he incurred, expenses to fund his travels. That might not have gone over well with his sister.

When he returned to London, he stayed at the residence of an acquaintance from his university days. Perhaps that person could tell us something as well—if Sir Nelson had mentioned anything he was concerned about regarding his work of the new exhibit.

With the new Egyptian exhibit still closed, the museum was not as crowded as it might have been. Upon arrival, I inquired at the main entrance about the possibility of meeting with the director of the museum.

"Lady Forsythe?" the clerk at the desk near the main entrance inquired.

"If you please. It is regarding an important matter."

I waited as he put through a telephone call to the director's office.

Sir Edward Thompson was the first director of the museum and distinguished for his studies of ancient manuscripts during his time as the head librarian of the museum.

My great aunt was acquainted with him and had suggested that I request his assistance when I arrived.

In consideration of his position and responsibilities, I hardly expected him to meet with me. An assistant perhaps. I was therefore surprised when the clerk returned the handpiece to the phone and personally escorted me to the director's office.

Sir Edward immediately rose from behind his desk.

"It is indeed a pleasure Lady Forsythe, although it would be preferrable under other circumstances. I received a call earlier from Lady Montgomery that you would be calling. How is her ladyship? She is well, I hope."

"Very well, thank you. When I left Sussex Square she was practicing her golf game."

He chuckled at that as he indicated the chair across the desk.

"A spirited lady to be certain, one I have long admired," he commented. "And now, you are obviously here about the matter that occurred yesterday in what should have been a celebration."

"Anything you might be able to tell me about the exhibit, Sir Nelson's work on it, and any others involved, could be very useful in resolving the situation."

We met for very near an hour, and Sir Edward was able to provide me the names of those who had assisted in assembling the exhibit.

It seemed that all were carefully selected and had worked previously on other exhibits, including ancient manuscripts that Sir Edward translated as well. Still, I asked for the names of those individuals. I then inquired about Mr. Hosni.

"Poor man," he replied. "He was quite upset, as you might well imagine, yet he insisted on returning to Sir Nelson's office this morning. There is still a great deal of work to be done on the catalogue for the exhibit."

We spoke of any unusual situations regarding the exhibit, difficulties perhaps, or anyone who might have been opposed to it. There were none that he was aware of.

"There was such excitement for the opening. It is very tragic that this has happened. There are also lectures that have had to be cancelled. And the loss of Sir Nelson is especially tragic. He was planning on returning to Egypt at the end of the month."

"He was staying with a colleague from his university days, I believe." I mentioned.

"Yes, Sir Anthony Fellowes. They were friends of many years. I can only imagine that this has been a dreadful blow for him."

I made a mental note of that. Perhaps Sir Anthony might be able to offer some insight. I inquired if I might be able to inspect the exhibit.

"It does seem as if the police have completed their inspection, although we are not allowed yet to re-open the exhibit. I am aware of your work in past matters, Lady Forsythe, and see no harm in allowing you access."

With that, his assistant was requested to escort me to the Egyptian room in the exhibit hall.

I thought of the previous day as we traversed the halls to the room that housed the Egyptian exhibit. There had been such excitement, then such tragedy.

When we arrived at the exhibit hall, I was somewhat surprised to discover the doors were not secured. There were only a half dozen stanchions with velvet ropes, the sort I had seen in theaters and opera houses, that blocked the entrance.

The clerk set aside one of the stanchions and opened the door for me. I thanked him and stepped inside the large room that had been transformed to resemble an antechamber in an Egyptian palace for the exhibit.

It was unusually quiet inside the room, closed off from visitors and attendants of the museum. I took out my notebook and pen.

I made notes of my conversation with Sir Edward, and began my walk about the exhibit. It was as I remembered it from the day before.

I made a diagram of the layout of the enormous room that included the stone table with the tall columns that lined the room, the display of canopic jars on a stone table, the glass-enclosed cases with ancient tools, another row of glass cases with gold jewelry and adornments that had been discovered, along with that carved statue of a cat that seemed to stand guard over it.

I made note of another display then, as I had the day before, I rounded one of twin floor-to-ceiling sandstone sculptures carved and painted with hieroglyphic text and temple ritual scenes. And, as I had the day before when Aunt Antonia had made that startled sound, I came face-to-face with that imposing statue of Ramses II.

As I approached that twelve-foot statue, my gaze was drawn not to the base where Sir Nelson's body had lain, but to the details of that statue—the intricate headdress he wore, the compelling features of the man who had once been Pharoah of Egypt, the powerful half-clad body with those carved markings on the shoulders. And what appeared to be a dark stain on one hand of the statue.

I had not noticed it the previous morning, but it was there now.

"Lady Forsythe?"

Startled, I turned and came face-to-face with Sir Nelson's assistant.

"Mr. Hosni," I remarked with more than a little relief. So deep had I been in my thoughts that I hadn't heard him enter the exhibit hall.

"I did not mean to frighten you. The door was open."

"The director was kind enough to allow me to see the exhibit once more," I explained. "I wanted to make my notes with the hope that we might be able to assist in the investigation into Sir Nelson's death."

"Yes, of course," he replied in heavily accented English. He glanced at the note book.

"You have made a drawing."

"It is often useful in making our inquiries."

"You are most skilled."

"I am not the artist in my family," I assured him. "My efforts are quite simple, however ..." I caught him staring at the statue with a frown on his face.

"Are you injured, Lady Forsythe?" he abruptly inquired.

That seemed somewhat strange. "Not at all."

He was staring at the stain on the statue's hand. "I would never touch an artifact." I assured him.

He had approached closer, and his frown deepened.

"This was not here before. It is not possible ..." He turned and stared at me. "The stain, it is blood. The curse of the Pharoah!"

"What curse?"

"The curse against whoever defiles the Pharoah. They will pay in blood!"

I assured him that I had not touched it.

"I just noticed it as well. I have no idea where it came from. Perhaps one of the museum staff ..."

"Do you have the amulet that I gave you?" he said with growing urgency.

I retrieved the medallion from my bag.

"You must hold it before you to protect against the curse."

It seemed pointless to explain that I had not violated anything, that I was only attempting to find information that might provide a clue in the murder of Sir Nelson.

Yet Mr. Hosni was most insistent and quite anxious. I held the amulet before me, and he began to speak in Egyptian.

"It is an ancient prayer to the gods to protect the keeper of the amulet from the anger of Ramses," he explained. He glanced at the hand of the statue.

"You must take care," he again cautioned.

"What is the meaning of the stain?"

"It means death to those who have defiled the statue."

"Sir Nelson?" Did he actually believe that Sir Nelson had been killed by an ancient curse?

"He was a very spiritual man. He respected our ways and gave prayers to the gods before he removed the statue. The blood is for the one who has done this dreadful thing. We must go now."

I was not one to question another person's beliefs, as I

returned the amulet to my bag and followed Mr. Hosni from the exhibit and back to the office he had shared with Sir Nelson.

It did seem that we were dealing with not only Sir Nelson's death, but a curse as well. The question was, was it a bad curse or a helpful one?

"The Eye of Horus will protect you," Mr. Hosni assured me as I sat at the small table with him and he poured tea.

I would have preferred something much stronger after the encounter in the exhibit room, if it could be called that, but graciously accepted the tea. I explained that I had questions about the previous day.

"I have heard of the work you do—most unusual for a woman," Mr. Hosni said. "I will help in any way that I can. As you see," he gestured to the desk, "there is still much work to be done for the catalogue that the museum wishes to provide. I was to assist Sir Nelson in this, but now ..."

He seemed genuinely upset and saddened by the loss of the man who had brought him from Egypt. I wondered what would become of him after the catalogue was completed.

"We were to return at the end of the month," Mr. Hosni replied. "Now ... You must forgive me, Lady Forsythe. His death is a great personal loss for me as well. I will try to answer your questions. Perhaps in that way I may be able to assist you in finding who did this."

"Was Sir Nelson upset about anything the past several days before the exhibit was to open?" I inquired. "Had anything happened that might affect the exhibit?"

He shook his head. "I know of nothing. Sir Nelson was most excited about it finally being ready for the world to see."

"Was there any disagreement among those he worked

with?" I asked. "Perhaps someone who didn't approve of his bringing the exhibit to London?"

I was aware there was controversy over removing artifacts from other countries—that they did not belong to the person who discovered them, but should remain where they were found.

"As I told you, Sir Nelson was highly respected among those in Cairo and with those who worked with him. He was very respectful in what he was doing, and he promised to return the statue and the artifacts found with it to the people of Egypt, unlike the one that was stolen earlier."

I was aware that a much larger statue had been discovered and removed several years earlier. It had eventually made its way to London. But Sir Nelson's discovery had been an unexpected one in Saqqara, where it was found, and had included those unique gold artifacts.

"Did he ever speak of criticism or difficulty from any of the other archeologists?"

"If there was any such thing, he did not speak of it. It was not his way."

"There are many gold pieces in the collection. Have you made certain that nothing is missing?"

"With the permission of the director, I worked through the night to make certain that everything was still there.

"Who would want to harm Sir Nelson?" he asked. "And then leave everything as it was when we completed the exhibit?"

Who indeed? Unless he came upon someone unexpectedly who was attempting to steal something from the exhibit and was caught in the process.

Yet, the museum was well secured at the end of the day, and guards were posted as there were a great many valuable pieces—

other statues, paintings, rare books, in other exhibits that could bring enormous profit from someone willing to take the risk of being caught.

Except, according to Mr. Hosni, there was nothing missing.

"When did you first work with Sir Nelson?" I inquired.

Mr. Hosni's expression softened. "Many years ago. I was hardly more than a boy. I was hired to accompany him on his first trip. I had no family and had been living on the street. The pay was only a few coins each week, but more than a child ever had.

"Because I had no family, I stayed with him and traveled to the other places that he had traveled. I came to England with him, and he arranged for me to study your history and your language. I returned with him to Cairo. I was with him when he discovered the chamber that the statue was in with the other artifacts."

It was a story not unlike Brodie's.

"What of his nephew?" asked. "Did he have contact with him?"

"He attempted many times upon our return to England. It seems there was some difficulty there. Mr. Sutcliffe came to London only days before."

"Before?"

Mr. Hosni nodded. "Sir Nelson spoke of it. He was not expecting it. He did not speak at length of it, but I sensed that it was not a pleasant meeting."

Family relations. I understood how difficult they could be. But just how difficult?

Sir Nelson's nephew, John Sutcliffe, and his family lived in Twickenham, where he was a teacher and private tutor. I thanked Mr. Hosni for the information.

"You will continue with your investigation?" he asked. "Even with what I have told you about the curse, and the stain we saw?"

"Sir Nelson was my friend as well," I replied. "I'm not afraid, and we will find the person who did this. What will you do now?"

"There is the catalogue to finish—that will take some time. After that is completed ... I do not know."

I left the office he had shared with Sir Nelson. I did feel such sympathy for him. He was in a foreign country, albeit one that he had lived in and been educated in as well. Still, he had lost a friend in the man who had taken him from the streets. As I knew only too well, such bonds ran deep, and he obviously felt that loss profoundly.

I was deep in thought, already making my mental notes about our conversation as I turned down the long hallway the led from the office. I might have run into the man if I hadn't suddenly looked up.

He was obviously one of the museum workers, dressed in a work shirt, cotton trousers and boots as he pushed a handcart, the usual sort one might find in the museum as exhibits were added to or changed.

The man ducked his head so that it was impossible to see his face, and continued on his way with a slight limp.

I returned to the office on the Strand after leaving the museum.

I had no sooner stepped down from the coach and greeted Mr. Cavendish when Brodie appeared and held over the driver. He gave him the destination of the Bow Street Police Station and we both climbed aboard.

"I was able to persuade the chief inspector to delay charges against Howard Carter for a few days," he explained.

He was also able to arrange for us to meet with Mr. Carter, our present destination, in an attempt to learn any information he might be able to provide that could be helpful in finding the murderer.

"Wot were ye able to learn at the museum?" Brodie asked.

I hesitated to tell him what Mr. Hosni believed about the discovery of the stain at the statue of Ramses II that wasn't there the day before.

Brodie was not a religious person, as far as I knew. He had never mentioned such, nor had we discussed it prior to our marriage. I suppose, for some, that would be considered an enormous error and we would be considered heathens.

Yet, the appearance of a stain on the statue might have the effect of convincing one of such things. I decided on a simple explanation.

"I spoke with both the director of the museum and Sir Nelson's assistant, Mr. Hosni. It seems that nothing was found to be missing from the exhibit. Either the murderer was interrupted as the exhibit was about to open, or the intended purpose was not robbery."

Much like the police investigator he once was, Brodie listened, a frown on his face as I eventually worked my way toward explaining what Mr. Hosni and I had discovered this morning.

"There was a peculiar mark that I noticed on the statue," I casually added.

"A mark?"

"It was more of a stain of some sort that wasn't there before."

"Wot sort of stain?"

And here we were with my best intentions, I thought, choosing my next words carefully.

"Mr. Hosni seemed to think that it might be blood."

Brodie was thoughtful. "It might have been left when Sir Nelson was attacked, if he attempted to fight off his attacker."

"It wasn't there yesterday."

That dark gaze met mine across the interior of the coach.

"Wot are ye saying? That someone else put it there afterward? For what purpose?"

I made an offhand gesture with a wave of my hand. "It's possible that it has something to do with the curse."

Those dark brows angled sharply as we arrived at the Bow Street station. Due to the other matter at hand—speaking with Howard Carter—I was spared his reaction, at least for the time being.

We signed in with the constable at the main desk. Brodie gave him the information that C.I. Graham had approved for us to meet with the prisoner. We were told to wait while paperwork was verified.

"Right yer are, Mr. Brodie," the man at the desk finally acknowledged as he motioned for another constable and gave him instructions to escort us to the holding section.

As we followed him, I caught the distinct change in Brodie as he returned to one of the places where he had once worked, and the frown that came with it.

We eventually arrived at the adjacent building where prisoners were detained until they were formally charged, then moved on to other facilities to await their court date.

"Mr. Brodie and guest to see the prisoner, Howard," he told the man at the duty station.

I caught the curious look the man gave me. It was obvious not many women came to visit.

Here again, approval for the visit was noted. Brodie turned to me.

"If ye should want to remain here ...?"

I assured him that I wanted to see Mr. Carter as well. We were asked to leave anything we carried with us with the constable at the duty station.

Brodie had left his revolver and the knife he always carried at the office, in anticipation of our meeting with Mr. Howard.

He gave me that look, one of several that I knew quite well.

"It will be returned," he assured me with a look at the constable to confirm it.

I retrieved the revolver he insisted that I carry. There hadn't been time to tuck it away at the office.

I handed it to the man at the desk, the one with the startled expression.

"Blimey! You carry this around, miss?"

I smiled. "And I am most proficient."

"Can we get on with it?" Brodie reminded him.

We were escorted to one of several holding cells down an adjacent hallway. I heard the key in the lock, and the cell door opened.

"People here to see you," the constable announced.

Howard Carter emerged out of the looming shadows inside the cell with only a single overhead light that blinked on and off. He blinked as well, as he recognized me.

"Lady Forsythe?"

Brodie explained the reason we were there and that we were making inquiries into the case.

"I do wish there was something I could tell you about that day," he said as he sat on the cot against the wall, while I sat in the other piece of furniture he was allowed, a straight-backed chair. Brodie stood and leaned back against the inside wall.

"Anything ye might be able to tell us?" he inquired. "Anything ye might have seen or overheard, anything out of the ordinary."

Howard Carter shook his head. "There was so much going on that day, last-minute deliveries from the area where the artifacts were stored, coordinating with staff to have everything in place for the opening of the exhibit ..."

"Was there anything Sir Nelson mentioned?" I asked. "Perhaps something about the exhibit. Was anything missing?"

Once again, he shook his head. "Everything was in quite a bit of chaos, what with those last items arriving that needed to be placed inside the room and all the last details. I checked everything against the list. Nothing was missing."

"Was there anyone about who shouldn't have been?" Brodie inquired.

Howard was thoughtful. "Not that I was aware."

That coincided with what the director of the museum had told me earlier.

"What about the workers who brought the additional artifacts from storage?" I asked.

"There were four, all on staff with the museum. I recognized them from another exhibit I had assisted with recently." He looked over at Brodie.

"Why am I here? They won't tell me anything."

"According to the information they have, ye were the last to have contact with Sir Nelson."

"They cannot possibly think that I had anything to do with his murder!" he exclaimed. "I respected him and worked with him the past two years when he returned to London."

"Did he mention anything about the curse associated with Ramses II?" I continued.

"It's fairly well known about dishonoring the dead," he

replied. "There's always a curse or two associated with archeology in Egypt. Sir Nelson was aware, but put no stock in it. I suppose one cannot, or nothing would ever be brought to museums."

"What about the dagger?" I asked. "Was it part of the exhibit?"

"It was part of the exhibit, displayed in a glass cabinet. It had been found with the statue of Ramses II according to Sir Nelson."

For those who believed in them, it might be proof of the curse.

He looked from Brodie to me. "What will happen now?"

Brodie explained that the police would continue with their investigation, while we did the same.

"I must remain here?"

"Mr. Brodie has made certain that the charges against you won't be formally read for several days. In that time, we will do everything we can to find the person responsible."

Howard slowly nodded. "It would seem that all I can do is wait."

I reached out a hand to comfort him. He looked very young and somewhat forlorn.

"We will succeed." I told him and asked if there was anyone he wished us to take word to about the situation.

"My father," he replied. "He will be quite upset about this. He calls my fascination with archeology a ridiculous folly, yet I would not want to worry him or my mother."

I took out my notebook and pen. "If you wish to send a note to them, I will see that it is delivered."

"I would appreciate that very much, Lady Forsythe."

He penned a brief note for his parents, explaining that he was working long hours at the museum and would be staying with a friend while he completed a work project at the museum. He handed it to me.

"I do appreciate everything that you are doing," he told Brodie. "And you as well, Lady Forsythe. You are acquiring quite the reputation for solving crimes." He continued to hold my hand for a moment longer, then laughed nervously.

"I do believe the situation is in good hands," he added.

I retrieved my revolver as we left the holding area at Bow Street.

"The Mudger, Mr. Brimley, and now Mr. Howard Carter," Brodie commented as we found a driver. "Ye do seem to have a way with them."

I looked up with some surprise.

"Ye have them fallin' at yer feet, including the hound. And the worst of it is, ye seem completely unaware."

"Whatever is your meaning?" I replied with wide-eyed innocence.

"Ye use yer woman's charms, as ye did on that poor lad."

"Woman's charms?" I replied with more than a little amusement.

"Ye know well enough wot I'm speakin' of. Yer intelligent, well-spoken, and caring in yer way."

"Why, Mr. Brodie, I do believe that you are jealous."

He scoffed at that. "I dinna have time, and there has never been a woman who deserved it."

"Never?" I asked, most curious.

That dark gaze met mine. His expression was equally dark and quite wicked.

"Well, perhaps *one*." He conceded. "What of yer visit with her ladyship? Was she able to provide any information regarding Sir Nelson?"

I managed to control my amusement over his last comment about my 'woman's charms.'

"It does seem there was some difficulty in Sir Nelson's family when he decided to pursue his explorations in Egypt. There is his sister and his nephew, who were apparently put out about it and the fact that most of the family wealth went to finance his explorations over the past several years."

"There might be something there," Brodie commented. "It could be useful to pay a visit to the man. Do ye have the nephew's name and whereabouts?"

I acknowledged that I did.

Before leaving Bow Street, Brodie asked to see the dagger that had been retained as evidence in the murder.

"Back at it, Mr. Brodie?" an older constable inquired as we were shown to the room where evidence was stored. It was much like a locker area at the German gymnasium, with rows of locked drawers in a cabinet that filled one wall.

"In the matter of a private investigation," Brodie replied as Constable Hughes checked the log book, then escorted us to the far wall where more rows filled another cabinet. Each drawer was labeled with the case name and number.

"More's the pity. It's different here since you left, but Mr. Graham is a good man," he added of the Interim C.I. He pointed to the cabinet

"All of this will be moved to the new building when it's ready. And here it is, Lawrence, case number 287." He opened the drawer and removed the gold dagger with a cloth wrapped around the handle. He laid it on a nearby counter for us to inspect.

"I'm usually required to stay when someone makes such a request so there's no tampering with evidence. However, in your case, Mr. Brodie, I've no concern in that regard. You know your way about these things."

With that Constable Hughes left us to our examination of the dagger.

It was approximately ten inches long, made entirely of gold. Intricate figures and script had been etched into the gold handle, with traces of dried blood on the blade. I recognized some of the characters from my travels to Egypt.

"It appears this might have been part of the funerary items to protect Ramses on his journey into the afterlife."

A highly valuable artifact that had been left behind by the murderer. What did that tell us?

When we returned to the Strand, Mr. Cavendish had received a message for Brodie. He was to meet the illusive Mr. Brown that afternoon at a designated location.

"Where would that be?" I asked, uneasy that the message had been specific that Brodie was to go alone.

"He's not of a mind for me to share that."

I didn't usually ask for specifics in such things, but I was uneasy with the arrangement.

"I told ye, I am far more valuable to him alive. And if he has information that might be useful, it would help resolve the case. Young Mr. Carter would be appreciative of that," he pointed out.

He kissed the back of my hand as he prepared to leave for his meeting.

"I'll be careful as church mice. And yerself?"

I might have pointed out that I wasn't worried about the mice. I didn't.

"Do you have your revolver?" I casually inquired.

He patted the front of his coat. "Always."

"I'll contact Sir Anthony." I commented as I waited with him for a driver. "He may be able to tell us if there was some incident, or a conversation he had with Sir Nelson that might tell us something."

"Be careful," he told me as a driver arrived. "It's already late in the afternoon."

"I'll take the hound with me." That brought the usual reaction, although I must admit that after our previous inquiry case it did seem that Brodie was coming around to the possibility that Rupert was well worth his keep. I had even caught him slipping the hound a biscuit one evening after we'd eaten at the public house.

And once more, he told me. "Be careful and dinna be about late."

I assured him that I would on both counts.

After he had set off, I had Mr. Cavendish take Howard Carter's note for his parents to the local messenger office. I made a telephone call from the office to the auction house at St. James with the hope of meeting with Sir Anthony Fellowes.

"Such a dreadful situation," he responded. "I am expecting a delivery and cannot leave until it arrives," he explained.

I assured him that I was pleased to meet with him at the auction house. I left a note for Brodie and locked the office door.

Mr. Cavendish waved down a driver as I reached the sidewalk at the bottom of the stairs. He did manage to navigate most efficiently on that rolling platform after losing both legs some years before in an accident aboard a cargo ship.

He was also the stalwart companion to Rupert the hound. Together they navigated the streets of London quite handily.

"Is there a message for Mr. Brodie when he returns?" he now inquired.

"I left a note on the desk upstairs. I'll return here after my meeting," I explained.

"He'll not like you going off on you own, miss," he reminded me, like the good friend he had become.

"It's still early in the day, Mr. Cavendish. I have the revolver he gave me; I'll be quite safe."

I whistled for the hound.

Six

I WAS FAMILIAR WITH ST. James's Street. The shops included the exclusive haberdasher to the royal family, an art gallery that I had visited more than once with my sister, and the Cortland Auction House. I had attended the auction house with my great aunt when she had been on a campaign to sell off several pieces of rare furnishings that were several hundred years old.

An attendant met me at the door. I gave him my name and was escorted into the main auction hall, where rare pieces were being displayed for the auction that was to take place the following day. I told Rupert to stay.

I had not met Sir Anthony Fellowes previously; however, there was only one person who could possibly be the owner of the auction house. He was dressed in an impeccable suit with black coat and striped pants. With thinning grey hair, sharp features, and a satin neck scarf, he held a notebook before him and called out instructions to the staff as they wheeled in other pieces, presumably for the auction the next day that was being promoted on the framed sidewalk board.

The attendant made Sir Anthony aware of my arrival. He turned and nodded in acknowledgement and handed his notes to the man as several workers continued to set up rows of chairs with velvet upholstery.

"Lady Forsythe, good afternoon."

He was very much my same height as he held out a hand and greeted me, then with a look around at the activity among the workers said, "My office might be better suited for a private conversation."

His office was like the office of any other professional person, with an elegant mahogany desk and Louis XV table and chairs, and an impressive hammered-copper war shield on the wall behind his desk.

"Forgive me for being somewhat distracted," he apologized. "It's just that there is so much to do with the auction tomorrow." He smiled when he saw my interest in the shield.

"It was a gift from Sir Nelson. I have always been interested in ancient Egypt. He thought of it as a way of repaying me for staying with me when he returned from his trips abroad. I refused to accept any compensation from him.

"It was a way for old school colleagues to catch up on things in the world. Neither of us had married, so it was just two single fellows, and our work."

That smile again.

"I explained that I would keep it for him for his exhibition at the museum. I had not had time to send it over." He shook his head as he folded his hands before him.

"When he didn't return that night ... I had heard of course, through people we both knew. Such a dreadful situation. I thought of postponing the auction, but he would not want that, as the invitations were already out and it is a source of income."

"Did he have artifacts that he provided to the auction?" I inquired.

"No, he was very adamant that no piece he brought back would be sold for profit. Other than the shield, everything he found went to the museum."

I explained that Brodie and I had been retained as consultants by the MET, and we were assisting in attempting to solve the murder.

"Any way that I may assist, Lady Forsythe," he assured me.

I explained that in our past inquiry cases, those who had contact with the victim might provide clues, as well as reveal any difficulties that were known. Things like debts or any threats that might have been made could be helpful.

"I understand there was some difficulty between Sir Nelson and his nephew," I added.

"Sadly, yes. It was a long-standing issue that I was well aware of. Nelson spoke of it. I know that it bothered him deeply. He wrote to his sister and her son and attempted to contact them whenever he returned. They sent only cursory responses that hurt him deeply.

"His nephew came to London to meet with him just days ago. They met at my residence. There was quite a row. His nephew demanded that Sir Nelson take on the debt for supporting his mother, Nelson's sister. When he attempted to explain, including something about the original inheritance she was given, things became quite ugly."

"Did he make any threats against Sir Nelson?" I asked.

"More than once, and then the young man left. His parting words were quite chilling, considering what has now happened."

"What were they?"

"He told Sir Nelson that in one way or another, he would pay for what he'd done to his family."

That did seem ominous. And if the meeting between Sir Nelson and his nephew was as Sir Anthony described it, there might be a motive.

I asked if there was anyone else who heard the confrontation between them.

"Regrettably only myself. I don't retain a large staff of servants. The only man in my employ, my secretary who assists with my work, had the evening away." He was thoughtful.

"I warned Nelson to take care and be cautious. I offered to make a loan to him to cover his nephew's claims, but he refused to hear of it. He said that it would never be the end of it." He shook his head once more.

"And just as he was about to show all of London the marvelous exhibition at the museum after years of hard work. Such a great loss. So very sad."

There was little more Sir Anthony could tell me. After that dreadful confrontation, Sir Nelson's nephew had departed.

A great loss indeed, I thought. And that confrontation just before Sir Nelson's death?

John Sutcliffe had refused to have anything to do with final arrangements for his uncle. To say that he was apparently not grief-stricken was an understatement.

Nor surprised? I thought.

It did seem that, in spite of the difficult circumstances, a visit with John Sutcliffe was in order. Most definitely a prickly situation. Family relations could be difficult, as I knew only too well.

From the information Mr. Dooley had provided, I had learned that John Sutcliffe lived in Twickenham. I was aware of the location from previous travels with my sister to the countryside south of London.

It was only a forty-minute trip by rail, yet very much like traveling to a different country. The community had grown considerably over the past several years as business people, families, and others sought to escape the crowded conditions in the city, the lack of suitable housing, and the crime.

I had made my last trip with my sister from Waterloo Station. Unless the schedule had changed, there should be a train departing the next morning.

I left the warehouse district and easily found a driver for the return to the Strand, thoughtful on the ride over everything Sir Anthony had told me. The hound was a good listener.

Brodie had not yet returned from meeting with Mr. Brown. I updated my notes and the chalkboard with what I had learned from Sir Anthony. It certainly did appear that John Sutcliffe might have had a motive, considering that last argument and obvious difficulties over the years.

And the means was obvious, with that dagger that was part of the collection in the exhibit. However, that raised the question about opportunity.

Where there was a will, there was a way?

Brodie eventually returned. His meeting with Mr. Brown had provided information that might be useful.

It was no secret that even in our modern day and age there was still a thriving smuggling business, which Mr. Brown had personal knowledge of.

A contact from Brodie's past with the Metropolitan Police, he had provided valuable information in our last inquiry case.

He was a shadowy figure who quite literally lived in the shadows. And he was quite dangerous, according to Mr. Cavendish. It spoke to Brodie's past on the streets when he and

Munro were forced to do all manner of things in order to survive.

He had been forthcoming regarding many of those aspects. However, when I had asked questions about details of certain other parts of his past, he had simply replied that it was not for me to know.

"Ye went alone to the London Docks?" he pointedly asked.

I had hoped to avoid that bit of conversation—however this was Brodie.

"It was the middle of the day ..."

"Well into the afternoon," he pointed out. "And verra near dark, and ye know it doesna matter much the time of day for a crime to happen."

"You were not here at the time ..."

"Ye should have waited."

I had the distinct feeling that I was losing the argument.

"I had no way of knowing when you might return," I pointed out. "And I did learn important information ..."

"Ye could have learned this tomorrow when we both could have gone."

"The hound was with me."

This was an old argument, a very old argument.

"Sir Anthony has the auction tomorrow, and there would be no opportunity." Not precisely the truth, however when navigating a conversation with Brodie, other measures were often required.

By the expression on his face, he wasn't convinced, but he didn't argue the point further.

"There is a train that leaves for Twickenham at ten o'clock in the morning from Waterloo Station," I continued. "I should like to question Sir Nelson's nephew, as there apparently was some difficulty between them, and he was in London quite recently.

"And you should know that I did have the revolver with me when I went to call on Sir Anthony Fellowes," I added for the sake of argument, not being one to let a thing go, particularly where I could win that argument.

He shook his head as he took another swallow of whisky.

"Ye will be the death of me, Mikaela Forsythe."

"None too soon, I hope," I replied with a smile. "We do have a case to solve."

We went over the rest of what we had each learned that afternoon.

From Mr. Brown he had confirmed that there was an extremely lucrative '*business*,' as the man described it, in stolen artifacts that were smuggled into the country from time to time, and sold to a well-placed gentleman.

"How might that be connected to Sir Nelson's murder?"

"There is a possibility that not everything he brought back with him made it into the exhibit at the museum."

"Are you saying that he might have illegally sold artifacts?" I found it difficult to believe of the man I knew.

"Ye did learn that he spent most of the family fortune on his expeditions, and by what ye told me of yer meetin' today, there were financial difficulties in the family. It is something to be considered."

"Did Mr. Brown know the name of the gentleman?"

Brodie shook his head. "The man is no fool. It would jeopardize some of his own business dealings if it was learned that he had given the name to me. But it does provide a different aspect to the case."

Was it possible that Sir Nelson had been involved in such

an enterprise? And that something might have gone wrong in a transaction he made?

I hated to think it. Yet, it was possible.

"We need to look at the guest list for the opening of the exhibit," Brodie said. "There might be something there that will provide a clue."

We had discussed the need to make a trip to Twickenham to speak with Sir Nelson's nephew. Brodie agreed that the circumstances of his visit and the argument that had followed was most suspicious.

"What about your visit with Mr. Hosni?" he asked.

"He appeared to be very upset by the events. Sir Nelson had helped him in so many ways, and it is difficult to believe he had anything to do with the murder of the man who sponsored him upon his arrival in England and assisted in his education here."

"Yer woman's instinct?" Brodie inquired.

I let that comment pass. Yet, my instinct did tell me that neither Mr. Hosni nor Howard Carter had anything to do with Sir Nelson's murder. There was no motive.

At least none that we were aware of yet.

There was something else I wanted to discuss with Brodie. It was part of this new aspect of our relationship, and there had been no opportunity earlier as he was off in one direction and I was off in another.

I poured us both another dram of Old Lodge.

"It seems that Lily has decided that she wants to be a private inquiry agent."

"Not an actress this week?" Brodie replied.

"She is most serious about it and you know how very intelligent and clever she is. And she has made some minor contributions in the past. She could be quite good."

He shook his head. "'Tis not a profession for a young woman with the sort of people she'd most likely encounter."

"It does seem as if she has made up her mind."

"She is too young to make that sort of decision."

"She is not a child."

"And ye didna object? Or in the least point out that she should choose something more appropriate?"

Something more appropriate? This was not going at all well, I thought, as I took another swallow of whisky and gathered my thoughts.

"The entire purpose in bringing her to London was to provide her a better future, more opportunities other than the streets," I pointed out.

"The purpose in bringing her to London was to provide her an education," he continued. "The work we are called upon to do is not a better future for the girl. Best she should get her education as ye promised, then a position in a lady's shop or as a lady's companion," he suggested.

Shop clerk? Lady's companion?

Neither suited her, with her stubbornness and temper, not to mention her rather colorful background. She wouldn't last a week in either position.

Note to myself: Choose my moments better to discuss such things or ... not at all. I chose to drop the subject. He did not.

"Or perhaps a position as a teacher or tutor, as Miss Mallory," he added. "That would be more appropriate."

As if that settled the matter.

I had simply wanted to inform him of the conversation as we shared other things about Lily and the boy Rory, whom he was especially fond of from another investigation. And it would perhaps have been better to let the matter rest, but I was not of a mind to do that.

"More appropriate?" I replied. "For a young woman?"

"Ye know my meanin'."

I was afraid that I did.

"She is not like other young ladies," I pointed out. "She has had different experiences and is quite use to making her own decisions and surviving until now quite well."

"She will change her mind by the week next," he pointed out.

"Perhaps, but I feel that we should support the decision she makes."

"For work as an inquiry agent?"

"Yes, if that is what she chooses." I felt my cheeks grow warm.

"She is not the same as yerself, and dinna look at me that way. She is young and could do much better."

I hadn't realized that I was looking at him that way. However, if it worked ...

"For a woman, you're saying."

It was a frequent topic of conversation, and the moment I said it, I knew the reaction I would get.

There was a French word I had read recently that came to mind—*chauvinist.*

The French had nothing over a stubborn Scot.

I slowly set my glass down as I recalled something my great aunt had once told me when dealing with certain people, most particularly a man.

"For certain they can be most aggravating creatures. However, there are some aspects that are most pleasant. The key to it all, it would seem, my dear, is to pick your battles."

I hadn't intended for this to be a battle. However ...

"The train leaves from Waterloo station at ten-thirty in the morning for Twickenham," I informed him, quite calm as I gathered my notebook and bag that I always carried.

"Aye," he said in that distracted way, the conversation obviously at an end as far as he was concerned. He rose from the desk and removed the revolver that he always carried from the waist of his trousers, and put it in the drawer of the desk as I went to the door.

"Good night, Mr. Brodie."

I thought better of it, for just a moment, then slammed the door.

Seven

I HAVE no way of knowing if Brodie attempted to follow me the night before, as I made my way to the sidewalk below the office and quickly found a cab. He did not appear at the door to the townhouse.

Nor was there a telephone call afterward, to inquire if I had arrived safely. Far better that there wasn't, I thought, with what I would have told him regarding his comments about proper young ladies. It might very well have destroyed the telephone.

As it was, I rose early this morning and quickly dressed for the trip to Twickenham.

Mrs. Ryan was mostly silent as she provided breakfast. She was quite fond of Brodie, in spite of the fact that she was Irish and he was not.

"Was Mr. Brodie working late on a case?"

I say, *mostly* silent. I merely nodded and asked if she would call for a cab.

Twickenham was in the south of London, with no direct connection from Mayfair, requiring a driver for the ride to Waterloo Station.

In spite of morning traffic about the city, we made the trip to the rail station in good time.

I paid the fare and navigated the crowded station to one of the ticket windows, purchased my ticket, then made my way to the platform for my train.

I had no idea if Brodie would be there, and so be it, I thought. I was more than capable of speaking with John Sutcliffe if he was willing to meet with me.

The announcement was made for passengers to board the train, and I made my way to the gate.

"Mikaela."

I would have recognized that voice anywhere, in spite of the clamor from the crowd of passengers that brushed past, eager to board the train. And in spite of the fact that I had convinced myself he would not be there and I did not care if he wasn't.

"Mr. Brodie," I stiffly replied as I presented my ticket to the attendant, and stepped into the rail car.

The trip by rail was short, with no need for a private compartment. I took a seat in the passenger car with the aisle between the rows. The car was crowded, and he took a seat a handful of rows past.

I had made my notes the night before in my notebook with information we had learned that day. I spent the duration of the rail trip, going back over them.

Brodie made no attempt to engage in conversation. The distance between would have been awkward. Yet several times I looked up to find him watching me with that dark gaze.

It was late morning when the train pulled into the rail station that served Twickenham. I put away my notebook and pen, and rose to depart the rail car. As I entered the aisle, he was there waiting for me to go before him. I quickly moved past and stepped down from the car.

Twickenham had grown from a village into a bustling town since my last visit to the country by way of the ferry on the river.

Working people with families, who could not find adequate places to live in London, chose instead to live here and travel by train to work in London proper.

It was Saturday, and, in spite of the late morning hour, those who waited at the station for the return trip to London were a mix of well-dressed couples, young families, and several young men from the local cricket club in their uniforms.

I found a station attendant and inquired about a driver. I was directed to the far end of the platform where I was told a man could be hired.

I heard a warning shout, but it came too late as a baggage cart careened wildly down a ramp toward me. There was no time to escape as it barreled toward me.

"Mikaela!"

I heard my name then a hand closed around my arm, and I was pulled out of the path of the cart as it swept past and crashed into another cart on the platform. Suitcases, valises, and a hat box scattered to the deck where I had stood only seconds before.

"Are ye all right?"

It took me a moment.

"Did it hit ye?"

"I'm all right."

"Are ye certain?"

A station attendant rushed toward us as two porters ran past to the wreckage of the luggage cart.

"Are you all right, miss?"

I assured him, and Brodie once again, that I was all right, as the two porters righted the cart and began to retrieve the scattered bags and boxes amid passengers who had gathered round.

"I don't know how that happened," one of the porters commented. "I set the brake on the cart myself."

Brodie and I exchanged a look.

"Perhaps there is something to that curse," he commented.

I wasn't inclined to believe in them, in spite of our earlier conversation.

"We will need a carriage," Brodie informed the station attendant.

The man moved quickly ahead to the carriage gate and signaled a driver. I stepped up into the carriage. Brodie stepped in after and gave the driver the address I had been given for John Sutcliffe.

Brodie glanced at me from time to time, a frown on his face surrounded by that dark beard, as we rode through the town of Twickenham, past the busy marketplace where customers gathered, and streets that spread toward the Thames.

We eventually reached the Green and the driver turned down the east side that was lined with sets of two cottages separated from the next two by a narrow path.

"Number Ten," he announced as he pulled the carriage to a stop.

Brodie stepped down and paid the fare. He asked the driver to wait. Then he returned and escorted me up the walkway to the cottage at Number Ten.

"Given wot ye learned about the last visit from his nephew, it may be a verra short meeting."

He was right of course.

Family relationships could be most difficult, if Sir Anthony's description of the encounter was any indication.

Brodie pulled the bell cord at the entrance to the cottage.

The door was opened by a woman somewhat older than myself and obviously not a servant by the cut of her gown. She was of medium height, with dark hair pulled atop her head, grey eyes, and pleasant features.

Brodie introduced us and asked if Mr. Sutcliffe was available.

"Consultants with the police?" she repeated with a startled expression.

"What is it, Kate?"

A man approximately Brodie's age appeared from an adjacent room. He was dressed in work clothes that were stained with dirt, a gardening implement in one hand, a perturbed expression on his face.

The woman repeated who we were.

"We're here in the matter of yer uncle's death," Brodie explained.

"I have nothing to say," he snapped, the words as blunt as that gardening tool.

"Ye made a visit to London and spoke with him two days before the ... incident," Brodie added. "Ye may speak with us or Chief Inspector Todd of Scotland Yard."

John Sutcliffe eventually nodded to the woman, who appeared to be his wife.

"You may ask your questions, but there is nothing I can tell you," he tersely replied as we sat in the small tidy parlor.

"Ye made a visit to the residence of Sir Anthony Fellowes where yer uncle had been staying since his return," Brodie recounted what we knew. "It would seem that the meeting was not cordial."

"What are you saying?" Sutcliffe demanded. He was now on his feet and paced across the room to the stone hearth.

I added the rest of what Sir Fellowes had told us. "We were told that you made a certain request that he turned down,"

"That is correct," he replied almost defiantly. "A reasonable request, but he adamantly refused!"

"John?"

He turned as an older woman entered the room. She was of average height, yet there was a resemblance in the eyes and mouth to the man I had met on my first trip to Egypt.

John Sutcliffe explained who we were and the reason we were there.

"It is in the matter of his death."

The transformation was immediate in the look that came into her eyes, her mouth taut.

"What do you want?" she spat out. "You see how we live when we once had a fine house in London. But my brother sold it, sold all of it to pay for his expeditions. Our father was respected. We were from an old family. We should be living in London."

When her son attempted to excuse her, she refused to be quieted.

"My son is a respected teacher and works very hard, yet he has been forced to beggar himself to my brother in order that we might live a little bit more comfortably!"

"Mother ..."

She again refused to be silenced. "My brother is dead! And I am happy for it. No more humiliation, no more begging for what should have been mine."

She was hardly finished. "As for any arrangements to be made? He can rot in the street!"

"Mother, dear," John's wife had appeared and went to her mother-in-law. "Do come away." She looked to her husband with a pleading expression.

"I will not be silenced nor apologize," the embittered woman announced. "My brother is dead and I am glad for it. My only regret is that it was not sooner."

With that, Sir Nelson's sister swept from the room, her daughter-in-law in her wake.

"Ye were at the museum the morning the new exhibit was to open?" Brodie commented, in that way I had seen before as he left the obvious question unspoken and waited.

Sutcliffe's head came up, his expression taut, barely restrained. Would he deny it?

"I was there," he replied almost defiantly. "Yet, I was not allowed into the exhibit hall. I was told that was for invited guests only!"

"Did you see Sir Nelson that morning?" I inquired.

"I have already explained that I was not allowed inside the exhibit, Lady Forsythe," he repeated in a scathing tone. "Is this how you amuse yourself? A lady of position and obvious means."

"Be very careful, sir," Brodie reminded him, the warning less than subtle.

"I was acquainted with Sir Nelson Lawrence and simply wish to assist in finding the person responsible."

"Title and wealth, patronizing those less fortunate," he replied, undaunted by Brodie's warning.

"You will leave now." He turned to escort us to the door. "As you see, we live simply. We cannot afford appropriate arrangements." He was most adamant. "Nor do we have any care for it. He is dead. You have my mother's reply."

Our meeting was obviously at an end.

"That was most enlightening," I commented. "At least we won't have to wait for a carriage."

The meeting with John Sutcliffe had been brief but quite revealing.

"He was there the day of the opening of the exhibit, after that nasty confrontation with Sir Nelson," I commented as we returned to center of town as there were at least two hours until the next train returned to central London.

We found a public house that had once been a coaching inn very near the railway station. They were serving the midday meal along with several varieties of beer. A woman with an apron, who obviously worked there, greeted us and showed us to a table.

She was young and most cordial.

"Travelin' through, are you? We get a lot of people from the rail station." She then went on to tell us what was available. "We have ham and beans or chicken in the pot with vegetables. What will you have?"

We both chose the chicken and ale to drink.

Brodie was most quiet and thoughtful as we waited, while I took out my notebook and pen and made notes regarding our meeting with John Sutcliffe.

"It would certainly seem that he, Sir Nelson's nephew, had a motive," I commented as the food arrived. "His sister as well."

"Aye, perhaps."

"You're doubtful."

"The man obviously had enormous resentment against Sir Nelson, and the sister as well. Yet there is the matter of access the morning the exhibit was to open," he pointed out.

I saw his point. "Is it possible that someone else acted on Sutcliffe's behalf?"

"Anything is possible," Brodie conceded. "However, ye saw how the man lives on a teacher's pay."

I was not convinced. I knew how strong resentment could be. Brodie as well, for that matter.

We finished eating, and Brodie paid for the meal. We then walked the short distance to the rail station. We didn't have long to wait, as the early afternoon train arrived and we boarded.

This time of the afternoon the rail car was hardly crowded. There were no more than a dozen other passengers, spread throughout.

We found two seats opposite across the aisle near the door to the car, other passengers scattered throughout, including a woman and her young son, a man in a plain suit who wore glasses who might have been a bookkeeper, and a young woman in the usual attire of a maid. The train soon pulled out from the station toward central London.

"It might be useful to learn if Mr. Sutcliffe had any pressing debts," I commented.

"Aye, perhaps," he replied, continuing to watch the woman with the young boy.

He was thoughtful for the longest time, and it seemed that the silence of the evening before continued.

"The boy reminds me of Rory," I commented.

"Aye."

"Not so much in his appearance, of course, for all that Rory has red hair, but more in his manner, unable to sit still, asking dozens of questions," I added. "I would imagine that he is quite a handful, and perhaps stubborn."

"Determined to have his way," Brodie replied.

Was he speaking of the boy we both watched, or Rory Matthews?

I knew that days earlier, he had been to visit Rory, the boy orphaned in one of our previous cases.

Brodie had reason to believe the boy might be his. After that dreadful case, Rory lived with his grandmother, Lady Matthews. She encouraged the bond between them. I had no objections after my own childhood experiences. I knew only too well the sadness of loss, and the anger left behind.

Brodie continued to watch the young woman and the boy.

"He is hardly a boy now, although he acts as one," he quietly commented.

There was a faint smile at his mouth as the boy in our rail car left his seat and approached the man with the glasses and began to ask questions. Quite inquisitive it seemed. His mother's expression suggested it might be a frequent occurrence.

"It seems a decision must be made about his schooling," Brodie said. "He is an intelligent lad, and Lady Matthews was thinking of one of those private schools and then university."

"He is very fortunate," I replied. "She does seem to want what is best for him."

"It seems the lad is not of the same mind."

He had not spoken of any difficulty in that regard. I did wonder what the difficulty might be.

"He wants to be a pirate or perhaps a police constable?" I suggested with more than a little humor.

He was quietly thoughtful for the longest time.

"It seems that he wants to attend an academy, one of those private military schools."

Not exactly training to be a pirate, if there was such a thing, which I doubted. And obviously not a place where young men trained to be a police constable.

"He is most insistent."

There had obviously been a conversation about it. As I knew well, a private military academy often led one into the Queen's service.

"I explained that it was not for him, that he should do as his grandmother wanted and look to entering university when the time comes," Brodie continued. "It would provide him with an acceptable profession."

Now where had I heard that before?

"Acceptable?"

"Aye, perhaps a physician, lawyer, or businessman."

"Or a teacher, tutor, or lady's companion for a young woman?" It was too irresistible, considering our recent conversation.

He looked at me sharply. "It is not the same for a young man who must be able to support himself and perhaps a family one day."

"What of a young woman who is determined to make her way and support herself, rather than being dependent on someone else for her existence? We have seen too much of that in our past cases."

"It is not the same. And dinna look at me that way."

"It is the same. You want what is best for Rory," I pointed out. "It would seem however, that no matter what *you* might want, he will have his way."

I was not without sympathy.

Brodie had grown up on the streets after the death of his mother, surviving on the streets by whatever means necessary.

He wanted something better for Rory. It was understandable, and ironic that he should now be faced with a willful boy who was determined to make his own decisions even if Brodie disagreed.

"He took your advice in the matter?"

That dark gaze met mine. "He did not," he replied, somewhat tight-lipped

It did seem the shoe, or the boot in this case, did not fit

particularly well. It did, however, explain our conversation the previous evening.

"The lad is being stubborn. He said that he would enter the military academy or not at all."

Stubborn, determined to have his own way in the matter?

"It does seem as if you are at an impasse," I replied, and added, "Not unlike Lily's aspirations to become part of our inquiries when she completes her studies."

That did explain his adamant response that she must choose something more *appropriate* for a young woman.

That dark gaze narrowed. "I know wot ye are doing. Ye have a devious way about ye, Mikaela Forsythe."

There were times when it took time for a stubborn, old-fashioned Scot to come around.

"Then you will support his choice." I concluded the obvious. "And Lily's as well."

"Do I have a choice in the matter?"

I smiled to myself. Not at all.

We arrived back at Waterloo station in good time, and made the trip back to the office on the Strand by cab.

Mr. Cavendish met us with some urgency at the sidewalk when we reached the office on the Strand.

"Mr. Dooley sent round a man earlier, said you were to contact him when you returned."

"Has something happened?" I inquired.

"He didn't say, only that it was important."

Brodie and I immediately climbed the stairs to the office, and he placed a telephone call to Bow Street.

Urgent indeed. Mr. Dooley asked us to meet him at the director's office at the museum straight away.

Eight

"SIR EDWARD THOMPSON contacted me straight away when the body was found early this morning by museum staff."

Body? My thoughts raced as he escorted us through the museum to the now-closed Egyptian exhibit hall.

A police constable had been positioned at the entrance, to prevent anyone entering, as well as signage that stated the exhibit was closed.

"Stand aside," Mr. Dooley told him as we entered the exhibit. Lights were on inside, obviously from those who had entered earlier.

Mr. Dooley led us through the exhibit to a corner of the hall very near that statue of Ramses.

While I was not squeamish at viewing dead bodies—one did tend to lose that after seeing several over the course of the past three years—it wasn't the body so much as who it was.

"Oh, dear," I whispered, as I recognized Mr. Hosni.

He lay sprawled on the floor of the exhibit in a pool of

blood before a cabinet with a statue. At least part of him. He had been beheaded, eyes staring in that last moment.

"This body was found by one of the workers who was allowed inside this morning to finish cleaning," Mr. Dooley explained. "By the condition of the body, it would seem that it happened late last night or in the wee hours of the morning."

Brodie knelt beside the body, while I chose to look for any clues that might have been left behind. That is what I told myself, as I tried to block out the image of Mr. Hosni's body.

"The weapon?" Brodie asked.

"None found," Mr. Dooley replied. "But it would seem to have been a substantial one, considering the wound. Not something one usually sees, even when you were working cases for the MET."

"Aye," Brodie replied. "Any other wounds?"

Mr. Dooley shook his head. "Just the one."

Brodie continued to inspect the body. He checked the pockets of the jacket Mr. Hosni was wearing, along with searching for anything else that might be around the body that could provide some clue as to what Mr. Hosni was doing in the exhibit late at night or early in the morning, as Mr. Dooley had surmised.

Perhaps working on the catalog as he had told me? There did not appear to be a notebook or pen anywhere nearby.

Brodie stood and looked over at me. "Are ye all right?"

Anyone else would probably have run screaming from the exhibit hall at the gruesome sight, or in the very least fainted. I did neither.

I was only recently acquainted with Mr. Hosni through Sir Nelson.

He seemed sincere in his friendship with the man who had

brought him to London and provided him not only work, but an education as well.

He had been forthcoming after Sir Nelson's death in that same room. And ironically, he insisted I have the amulet that might have protected him.

I frowned as I stared at a sandstone bust atop the mahogany pedestal beside where Mr. Hosni lay.

"Wot is it?" Brodie asked.

"Unless I am mistaken that is Sekhmet," I replied as I studied the features of the bust that appeared, by the broken edge of the bust, to have once been attached to the rest of the statue.

"Most curious. It might mean nothing, of course."

"Who is Sekhmet?" Brodie asked.

"An Egyptian goddess. I've seen something very like this before."

"Ye believe it might mean something regarding the man's death?"

"Perhaps. There is someone who might be able to tell me more."

Mr. Dooley would see that the body was removed and some sort of arrangement made after the police surgeon had made his examination and written a report.

I did not look at the headless body again as we left. There were the dozens of questions, as there always were. The obvious—who had killed Mr. Hosni, and to what purpose?

Was it the same murderer who had killed Sir Nelson? That seemed most likely. Or was it someone else? For what reason? Considering the brutal method by which he had been killed, where was the murder weapon? And was there some meaning to his body being found where it was?

It was very near five o'clock in the afternoon when we returned to the office.

Sir William Flinders Petrie, whom I had met previously when he lectured at University College in London, had recently returned from Jerusalem.

He had done early field work at Stonehenge and established sequence dating as a method for determining the origin of ancient ruins. Afterward, he traveled to Giza and began his explorations there.

Sir William had published countless articles that had raised the awareness as well as interest in that ancient part of the world, and had fueled my passion to travel there. He was presently preparing to return to Egypt within the next few weeks.

I made a telephone call to Sir Edward Thompson's office at the museum. In spite of the dreadful turn of the day, I hoped to find him there. He might well know where I could reach Sir William.

"*Dreadful! Simply dreadful!*" the director exclaimed when I told him the reason for my telephone call.

"*Two deaths in as many days. And now rumors that the exhibit is cursed. I have no way of knowing when we may open the exhibit.*"

I did understand his concerns; however, solving the murders might well go a very long way to dispelling rumors of a curse. He was most helpful in that regard.

Sir William lived in Hampstead when he was in residence; however, with a short stay before departing once more, Sir Edward informed me that Sir William was staying at the Midland Grand hotel while presenting a lecture series before his return to Jerusalem.

Due to the weekend, he was not making his final lecture at the Egyptian Hall until the following Monday, then departing for the Continent. With the urgency of our investigation, I immediately placed a telephone call to the Grand and asked the clerk at the front desk to have a message delivered to him.

And we waited.

"You know the man?" Brodie asked.

"I met him once at University College. Aunt Antonia is a patron of his Egyptian Exploration Fund, which sponsors his travels there. He rarely returns to London."

In spite of what obviously had to be an extremely full schedule for him, I could only hope that he would return my telephone call.

It was very nearly seven o'clock of the evening when the telephone rang. He remembered our encounter and inquired about my great aunt. When pleasantries had been exchanged, I explained the reason I had contacted him.

"Yes, I had heard of the situation at the museum. Such a dreadful tragedy."

I briefly explained that Brodie and I had been called in as consultants to the case, and I would like very much to speak with him regarding questions I had.

In spite of what I could only assume was an extremely crowded schedule in such a short time, he agreed to meet with us at the hotel. He was having supper that evening with a donor to his Egyptian fund, but would be pleased to meet with us afterward.

Brodie and I returned to Mayfair where we both changed into something more appropriate for our meeting. There was just enough time to call for a cab for our meeting with Sir William Flinders Petrie at the Grand.

It was after ten o'clock in the evening when we arrived;

however, with the hotel's location near the rail station, there were a good many people about, late arrivals, or those staying in London for other purposes.

At the front desk Brodie announced our arrival and that Sir William was expecting us. He was still in the dining room with his guest, and asked us to join him there, in a message returned by a hotel clerk.

He was as I remembered him, quite handsome, with a full beard and that inquisitive gaze, a man who had accomplished a great deal in the field of archeology.

He stood as we arrived. His guest was just departing; however, a young woman remained. From everything I knew about Sir William, he was 'unattached,' as the saying goes. He had once commented in an article for the Times newspaper that his schedule and travel hardly allowed for marriage and family.

The young woman was pretty, with red hair and a soft blue gaze, and had a notebook and pen on the table before her. A kindred spirit!

He introduced her as his assistant, Hilda Urlin, who was a geologist with a strong interest in Egypt.

"She is most accomplished and I needed someone to catalogue all the information I have brought back with me. She makes sense of it all, while my efforts are hardly legible."

She was most pleasant and engaging. "I understand that you have traveled widely as well, Lady Forsythe," she commented. "I am hoping to make the trip to Egypt in the coming year, although my work here for Sir Wiliam and the fund keeps me chained to a desk and a typewriter."

A kindred spirit indeed. She was also working on a book she hoped to have published. I gave her my publisher's name for when it was completed, and encouraged her to contact him.

I introduced Brodie and explained the work we did, as well as our current assignment as consultants to the MET.

"I've read the cases you and Mr. Brodie have worked on," Hilda commented. "It must be exciting."

I agreed that it was at times, and often challenging as well, and now we were immersed in this latest case.

"Dreadful tragedy," Sir William commented as we sat at the table. "I was to meet with Sir Nelson before leaving London regarding his latest endeavor. I heard the news of his death, of course. Word travels quickly about such things."

Brodie explained that there was now a second murder along with a brief mention of the manner of death. If I expected Sir William or his assistant to be shocked or horrified at the particular circumstances, I was surprised.

"I had met his assistant, Mr. Hosni, previously," Sir William commented. "He seemed very devoted to Sir Nelson." He turned to me.

"You said in our earlier conversation that you needed my assistance with something. How may I help you?"

In addition to the manner of death, I explained the location that Mr. Hosni's body was found, in front of the pedestal stand with that sandstone bust. I had made a sketch of it once we returned to the office and showed it to him now.

"Ah, yes. Sekhmet, a very powerful Egyptian goddess."

"What can you tell us about her?"

According to Sir William, she was a goddess first discovered from writings discovered in explorations of the Old Kingdom. She was supposedly the daughter of the sun god Ra, and drawings as well as papyrus referred to her as the goddess of war and destruction. Others showed her in the appearance of a cat as the goddess of healing.

"What might the significance be that his body was found at the foot of the pedestal?" I asked.

"Revenge, if one believes in such things."

"Revenge against whom? For what?"

"There are those who believe it is revenge for removing artifacts from Egypt," he went on to explain. "I have encountered such things before, yet I am well and planning my next trip there."

"And the manner of death?" Brodie inquired.

"It was very important to Egyptians for the body to be protected and cared for before the journey into the afterlife. What you have described would appear to be an execution—the head severed from the body. To the Egyptians and their priests, it was a way to punish a person and prevent him from making the journey."

"And now, in the Nineteenth Century?" I asked.

"Egypt is a very ancient land, and many hold to the old beliefs. That is what makes it fascinating, and at times dangerous."

"And what would their belief be when it came to protection against the goddess?" Brodie inquired.

"For those who believe in such things, the eye of Horus is a protective image, found on burial chambers, in ancient writings and carvings."

"An amulet?" I suggested.

Sir William nodded. "It is often worn for protection. I have seen it among those I work with when I'm there. Many still hold with the old beliefs."

I explained about the amulet that Mr. Hosni had given me that first day. He was surprised.

"It would seem the reason he gave it to you after Sir Nelson's death would be for protection against something he feared might happen. It doesn't matter whether you believe it. It matters only that *he* believed it."

And with good reason it would seem. But what did all of it tell us?

"What would be the symbolism of the gold knife?" I asked.

"A warning perhaps for those who believe in curses, death by a weapon that Sir Nelson had taken from Egypt," he replied.

"Revenge?" I suggested, which was the belief attached to the goddess Sekhmet.

Sir William nodded. "With what you've told me of Mr. Hosni's murder, it would seem that it might have been revenge against both of them.

If one believed in curses, I thought.

"What about the gold dagger?" I asked. "Is there some hidden meaning?"

"Gold was highly prized by the Egyptians," he replied. "It has been found on several sarcophagi, items found in tombs, even on walls. It symbolized one's status. What of the other weapon?" he asked.

"It wasn't found with Mr. Hosni's body, nor any other place in the exhibit," Brodie replied.

"What was Mr. Hosni doing there after the exhibit had been closed?" Sir William asked.

"He has been working on a catalogue of the exhibit for the museum. When I last spoke with him, he wanted to complete it."

He nodded. "So very sad. As I said, he was a good man. He understood the importance of these exhibits where others might come to understand the people. And most certainly it wasn't for plunder.

"Sir Nelson lived quite simply, and I'm told invested his own money when he traveled there. It is a sad and tragic loss."

It had grown quite late in the evening. I thanked Sir William for taking the time to meet with us and wished him success on his return to Cairo. And it was a pleasure to meet Hilda Urlin. As I said, a kindred spirit. I hoped that we might meet again.

I kept turning everything we had learned over and over in my mind on the return to the office, as did Brodie.

"It might be useful to check the inventory in the exhibit against the catalogue Mr. Hosni was working on to determine if anything is missing," Brodie suggested.

"Something the murderer might have stolen?" I replied.

"We need to find a motive."

"A simple robbery?"

"Perhaps." Brodie was thoughtful as we arrived at the townhouse.

"Two murders, the symbolism of the dagger and that funerary mask, and the way Mr. Hosni was killed as if it was an execution."

The question was, for what, though? Revenge, according to the belief in Sekhmet–a very angry goddess according to Sir William.

Or a robbery of valuable artifacts as Brodie seemed to suspect? All of that gold could be very tempting.

Yet, if not for robbery, then for what other reason?

The clues we now had, few as they were, might possibly lead in two directions as to motive.

I did wonder if Sekhmet's anger and the curse could be considered a motive. For someone who believed in such things and was carrying out acts of revenge ...?

We returned to the office on the Strand, even though it was late in the evening, so that I could update the board with what we had learned.

Nine

WE ROSE EARLY of the morning.

I had already decided that I would return to the museum with the hope of being able to find Mr. Hosni's catalogue for the exhibit, and compare it to what was actually in the exhibit. If anything was missing, that might tell us something.

Brodie was determined to see Howard Carter released from Bow Street. With Mr. Hosni's murder, it did seem that whoever had attacked and killed Sir Nelson was the very same person.

While I wasn't certain he would be able to persuade acting C.I. Graham to release him, I was grateful. I liked Howard Carter very much and felt that he had been caught up in this simply by that old saying, *in the wrong place at the wrong time.*

While Brodie seemed to be convinced that what had taken place was actually a robbery, he also wanted to speak with the illusive Mr. Brown. He had left word for him the day before, but there had been no response.

"I suppose if I told ye not to go, ye'd go anyway."

I didn't respond to that. He knew the answer.

"There are things that I am better at, and I will be perfectly safe. There are still constables at the museum posted at the exhibit hall," I pointed out.

He pulled a face, which in his case was more of a snarl.

"It will all be quite boring," I told him. "Comparing the catalogue notes with the artifacts in the exhibit. Not exactly something you're good at. Unless you're concerned about the curse. Remember, I do have the amulet for protection."

He scoffed. "'Tis not the curse. There is still a murderer out there."

He slipped his arms around me and pulled me close.

"Ye are important to me, Mikaela Forsythe."

"Important. Now there is a word to flatter any woman," I replied, angling my head back to look at him.

"Who would make notes for our inquiry cases? I suppose that might be important.

"And one can barely read your writing. Even Mr. Dooley complains of it, and he has no doubt had a great deal of experience when you were with the MET.

"Who would see that the electric and the rent is paid, not to mention the coal man?" I added.

His history for paying weekly or monthly bills in the past was usually to who ended up at the door to the office and demanded payment. Or more recently finding oneself suddenly in the dark with no fuel for the stove.

"Ye are a cheeky lass. Ye know well wot I mean," he replied.

"Of course, it must be most important that I make certain we always have a sufficient supply of coffee, not to mention my great aunt's whisky."

"*Spioraid,*" he said in Scots, his voice low in that way that always caught my attention.

"And what does it mean?" I asked.

"Spirited. Ye've got the devil in yer eye this morning."

I laid my hand against his cheek, his beard tickling my fingers. I knew where it came from, that need to protect what was his.

Yet, he also knew I would not sit idly by, cooling my heels, waiting for him to return. There were now two murders, and I refused to waste time while finding the person responsible.

"I want very much to find who did this," I explained. "Sir Nelson dedicated his life learning about Egypt and the Egyptian people, and he was most generous with his knowledge when he didn't have to be. He deserves to have the truth known, Mr. Hosni as well."

Brodie brushed the hair back from my cheek.

"The risks ye take."

"No different than the risks you take," I pointed out.

He kissed me again.

"Whether I want it or no, ye are part of me, lass, and this curse ..." He brushed my cheek with his fingers.

"It doesna matter whether I believe it or no, but wot others believe. Ye must promise to be careful. Perhaps ye should take the hound with ye to the museum."

Another surprise there.

It had taken him some time to accept Rupert, as he had never had a dog, or a pet of any kind for that matter.

Admittedly, Rupert was not the usual sort of pet most people had. He lived on the streets, his manners were appalling, and he came and went as he chose, usually with something quite disgusting in his mouth that he'd found.

Yet, he had an engaging smile when he wasn't gnawing on a bone, was fiercely loyal to Mr. Cavendish, and had proven himself most effective in protecting me on more than one occasion.

"I'm not certain the director of the museum or patrons would appreciate that. He might make off with one of their artifacts or offend one of the guests."

"Aye, he does have a peculiar appetite for things. But he has a special affection for ye, and I would prefer that ye take him with ye."

Prefer? To anyone else that might have sounded very much like a suggestion. Yet, I knew better.

Compromise. It was something I had never been good at, nor had Brodie, I had discovered. We were both learning our way around that.

I agreed to take Rupert with the provision there would be no objections from the director nor any of the staff.

"And you will be careful as well, in your meeting with Mr. Brown," I told him. "I don't trust the man."

I doubted that was Mr. Brown's real name, considering the profession he was in—noted smuggler, and leader of a somewhat notorious band of thieves that controlled certain *enterprises* on the streets of the East End.

"Aye, true enough, but we have an understanding," Brodie replied with a gleam in that dark gaze.

"What sort of understanding?" I inquired. I was certain it was something far more nefarious than merely information, as Brodie would have me believe.

He kissed me again in parting.

"Ye might say that I know where the bodies are buried."

Bodies?

Then he was gone.

I placed a call to Mr. Dooley and explained the purpose for another visit to the museum. He agreed to contact the director to make him aware so that I would have no difficulty.

I didn't bother to mention Rupert. There was a possibility

that he might not have returned from his usual morning tour of the Strand. However ...

It was midmorning when I arrived at the museum. I checked in at the desk at the main entrance and explained the reason I was there as a consultant to the investigation.

"We don't usually allow animals in the museum ..." the attendant politely informed me.

"Oh dear, of course," I replied. "You may remove him."

He gave the hound a long look. "I suppose there is no harm, as long as he doesn't disturb any of the displays."

I thanked him and we continued to the office Mr. Hosni had shared with Sir Nelson.

A constable was stationed outside. He nodded congenially.

"I've heard about yer work, and about that fellow," he gestured to the hound. "Is he on the case as well?"

Cheeky fellow.

There were no further comments as the constable opened the door and I stepped inside. Rupert followed, fascinated with new scents to be investigated.

Inside the office, I easily found the catalogue, still open on the desk where Mr. Hosni had obviously been working on it.

It did seem odd that he hadn't taken it with him to the exhibit hall where his body was found. Perhaps he had gone to the hall to verify one of the artifacts once more.

I sat at the desk while Rupert explored the office. There were three pages of entries with descriptions neatly printed for each one, with those check marks in the column beside it. Except for one, described as a Khopesh sword made of bronze.

I had seen pictures of such a sword in sketchings from inside Egyptian tombs. They were far different from English swords, much shorter, with a crescent-shaped blade for slashing and an outside edge for hacking. A formidable weapon indeed.

The drawings I had seen when I was in Egypt were from paintings on walls over three thousand years old, according to what Sir Nelson had described at the time.

It seemed that there had been a Khopesh in the collection he had brought back, except the absence of a check mark indicated something far different and had perhaps caused Mr. Hosni to return to the exhibit.

I searched the office for anything else that might seem unusual or out of place. I had previously noticed that Mr. Hosni was meticulous in his appearance and manner, and as I had observed, in his notes in the catalogue.

Yet there were items on the desk that seemed to have been moved, perhaps carelessly put back in place, along with a drawer that had not been completely closed by whoever had last been there.

I had worn gloves, something Brodie had once suggested as a precaution against disturbing anything in our searches. I eased the drawer open and carefully searched the files I found there. Once more, I recognized Mr. Hosni's precise printing on each file tab.

He had most certainly kept everything orderly here as well. I did notice that one of the files, marked as 'bills of lading,' was slightly askew as if it had been removed and quickly returned.

What might those tell me? I tucked the file under the tablet with those catalog entries.

It was possible that Mr. Hosni had found some discrepancy. And had then left the office with some urgency when he returned to the exhibit hall?

Or had someone else searched the office, forced to quickly leave when someone—perhaps one of the constables—had returned when they came on duty?

I had made a note about the missing sword in my notebook, along with a question about the disarray at the desk, something only someone who had previously met Mr. Hosni might have noticed. I gathered the file and the catalogue.

It seemed the only way to learn if anything was missing was to verify the catalogue against the artifacts on display, as Mr. Hosni had.

I thanked the constable outside the office, and made my way to the exhibit hall with the hound trotting alongside.

We received a few curious stares from guests, including one extremely alarmed patron. It might have been the tiny, fluffy dog she carried who set up a considerable fuss. The hound stopped, stared, and eventually followed me, with much persuasion and a somewhat stale biscuit left from our supper that night that I had thought to put into my bag before leaving the office.

The constable stationed outside the exhibit hall merely gave us a curious look. I informed him that I might be there a while.

He went off his shift at four in the afternoon and would let the man coming on know if I needed to remain longer. I thanked him and entered the hall and set to work.

Mr. Hosni had thankfully catalogued the display according to placement in the hall, beginning at one end of the large room. Otherwise, I might have been there for days going back and forth searching out individual pieces. I looked at the hound.

"Make yourself comfortable," I told him. "We will be here for a while."

'A while' turned out to be several hours in spite of the logical, methodical manner that the catalogue was set up. I had toured other exhibits previously.

Most catalogues in the case of ancient artifacts were often set up in time periods covered by the exhibit. However, this particular exhibit specifically covered the time period of Ramses II rule as Pharoah of Egypt, and it was limited to what Sir Nelson had discovered at the time.

Mr. Hosni had then created the catalogue to follow the flow of artifacts with signage from the early part of Ramses' reign, and in such a way to take the visitor through different parts of that early reign that included four sarcophagi and two stone caskets of those of high rank in society who had served the Pharoah.

There were tall clay jars painted with figures, gold utensils and jewelry, along with canopic jars, statues of important gods and goddesses, free-standing as well as in cabinets, hand-painted figures and boxes, and that sandstone carving of Sekhmet.

It was a bit daunting as I began with the catalogue in one hand and my pen in the other, while Rupert groaned as he stretched out on the floor and promptly went to sleep.

I had been at it for some time when I stopped to stretch against the stiffness in my back. I looked around for Rupert. He was still laid out just inside the entrance to the exhibit. I smiled.

"Worthless beast," I told him.

I glanced down at the watch pinned to my blouse. It was just after four o'clock in the afternoon. There was only a small section of artifacts left to verify, and I was determined to finish what Mr. Hosni had begun.

He had found a discrepancy between the shipping manifests and artifacts in that room, and I was determined to find it as well.

The section that was left contained those sarcophagi as well as the elaborately carved sandstone caskets, six canopic jars, and a hand-painted gold-inlaid box.

Everything was accounted for so far as I set off across the room for that last section of artifacts that also included that imposing statue of Ramses II.

There were fewer, if larger, artifacts in this part of the exhibit. It should take only a short amount of time to finish, even with the smaller statues and gold figures displayed that gave a visual impression of what the individuals in those sarcophagi might have looked like when alive.

There were two priests and two women depicted in the figures and on the sarcophagi. Possibly family members?

From Sir Nelson I had learned that members of royal families were often entombed together in those burial tombs in Egypt when each one died. It held with the belief that they would be reunited in the afterlife.

The carvings and paintings on the sarcophagi were fascinating, depicting scenes from that person's life, their position in the Pharoah's kingdom, as well as an oval cartouche on one that might have signified a royal relative.

I made notes in my notebook as well as verifying each artifact. There had to be something that would tell me more, I thought. Then I discovered that it appeared that the painted box with gold inlay was missing.

Was that what Mr. Hosni had discovered?

I went back through the hall, looking for the box that might have been placed elsewhere, but failed to find it. I returned to the location of the jars.

The exhibit had first arrived weeks earlier, and work had begun on the displays very soon after. No one else might have found the evidence, even if they were looking for it. Yet, I knew from pieces of china, vases, furniture, and swords in the sword room at Sussex Square, they had a tendency to collect dust if not cleaned or used regularly. Or stored away.

I learned that quite young, exploring my great aunt's residence that had stood for several hundred years. Admittedly, a few hundred years didn't compare with a few thousand, as in the case of the Egyptians.

By carefully moving first one jar aside, then another, I discovered the faint outline where the box had been.

It had been discovered some years before that hand-painted boxes often contained cosmetics, jewelry, and small figures of gods to accompany the dead person into the afterlife. It hardly seemed that it might be something worth stealing, let alone murder.

A sound came from where those ornately carved stone caskets were displayed. Massive in size, it had undoubtedly taken several men to maneuver them into place.

The figures that decorated them celebrated the person's life, the position that person held, and depicted the final journey.

They were beautiful, and I could imagine the weeks, months, perhaps years it had taken to carve those scenes.

It appeared that the lid of one had been pushed back.

Had it been jarred loose when it was moved into place for the exhibit? I tried to remember if I had seen that when I was there previously.

Was it possible that someone had moved it afterward ...?

The blow caught me at the back of my head in an explosion of light and pain, and then I was falling, a figure bending over me.

The last thing I was aware of was vicious snarling and someone screaming ...

Ten

"LADY FORSYTHE! CAN YOU HEAR ME!"

A voice somewhere nearby, as I slowly came out of the dark. My first thought was that it wasn't Brodie, but someone else.

"Do be careful, Lady Forsythe. You've taken a dreadful fall."

A fall?

I had been in the Egyptian room ...

There was an odd sound ...

The lid pushed back from the casket ...

A scream and the sound of ...

Rupert?

I abruptly sat up and immediately regretted it. It felt as if my head was twice its size and everything blurred before slowly settling back into place.

I was still in the Egyptian room. On the floor of the exhibit hall, to be more precise, with Sir Edward and two police constables bending over me.

"Did you see him?" I asked.

Anything more was going to take a few more minutes as I probed the back of my head where I discovered a large bump.

"I beg your pardon?" Sir Edward asked. "There was no one else about when Constable McLean came on his shift." He slipped an arm under my own as I pushed to my feet and stood.

"There was no one else." Constable McLean repeated. "There was just the bloody beast I found in here that wouldn't let anyone near until we were able to get a rope on him."

A rope? Anger was always a good tonic.

"He's with me ... Where is the hound?" I demanded, then lowered my voice.

The sound was quite painful.

"Where is he?" I demanded again.

"The constables turned him out onto the street."

"Bloody hell," I exclaimed. I could only imagine the chaos of that. And now Rupert was in an unfamiliar part of the city.

Bloody hell and a few other words that came to mind.

"Please do be careful, Lady Forsythe," Sir Thompson again cautioned.

I was attacked and no one was seen?

"What about the casket?"

He looked at me as if I might have taken leave of my senses. At the moment, I might have agreed.

"The lid on the one casket had been pushed back." Every word took an effort.

"Right yer are, miss," the other constable informed. "Why the devil would someone want to open a casket?"

What the devil indeed?

"Do come along, Lady Forsythe. You must be careful after the fall you've taken," Sir Edward insisted as he slowly escorted me to the entrance of the exhibit.

He was beginning to sound annoying.

"My notebook, please, and the catalogue Mr. Hosni was working on?" I asked.

Constable McLean handed them to me. "It might be best if you were to see a physician."

"It would be best for you to find me a driver," I informed him as I clenched my teeth against the throbbing at my head.

I slowly made my way from the exhibit hall, Sir Edward hovering beside me.

"I will need to contact Inspector Dooley," Mr. McLean said from my other side.

Of course.

"Be certain to mention that there was someone else there," I reminded him. I had not merely 'fallen,' as Sir Edward described it.

"You cannot mean that someone might have returned to the exhibit?" Sir Edward dithered beside me.

"That is exactly what I mean." I replied and resolved to add it to my notes. And who would have needed to attack me when he was discovered?

I needed to get back to the office and make my notes.

To say that we drew a fair amount of attention as the director escorted me from the hall and across the museum to the entrance along with Constable McLean, was an understatement.

I caught the whispers behind ladies' hands and the openly disapproving stares from men, which led me to another bruised thought. I could only imagine Brodie's reaction. He would 'have a fit and fall into the middle of it,' something I had heard my great aunt say more than once. Followed, I was certain, by a tirade about going off by myself in our inquiry cases. However, not precisely by myself, I thought.

And where the devil was Rupert? Caught with a rope and turned out?

Upon reaching the main entrance with that wide circular roadway beyond, Constable McLean went ahead and waved down a coach.

"Perhaps the constable should accompany you," Sir Edward suggested.

I suspected he was more concerned about my great aunt's sponsorship. I assured him that was not necessary as I gave the driver the address of the office on the Strand.

I glanced about, wincing in the process. There was no sign of Rupert. I climbed aboard, with my notebook and that catalogue safely tucked into my bag.

As we set off, I heard a familiar baying sound. There was only one creature who made that sound. Perhaps two, I thought of Brodie, as I signaled the driver to stop. However, that would most definitely be a snarl.

I opened the door of the coach and Rupert leapt inside and promptly dropped something at my feet and looked up at me expectantly.

It was a piece of fabric.

I thought that I might have imagined those sounds after I was struck. Yet, it seemed that I had not.

It did appear that the hound had attacked whoever had struck me, and the piece of cloth was quite bloody. I tucked it into my bag.

"Good boy."

"There is a theory by one of my former colleagues at King's College about head injuries," Mr. Brimley commented as he shone an irritating light into my eyes. I winced at the pain it caused.

"That an unevenness in the pupils of the eyes might indicate a brain injury," he continued. "It's most often seen among boxers who go at each other."

There was only silence from the person who leaned back at the edge of the desk, more specifically—Brodie.

"There have been some interesting studies from Edinburgh." Mr. Brimley concluded his examination and proclaimed me more or less unharmed, other than the knot on the back of my head.

"The Egyptians were quite proficient at studying brain injuries," he said as he tucked away that small hand-held light. "Including surgeries of the brain, while the patient was conscious," he added.

"Most fascinating. As for you, Miss Forsythe, you are most fortunate the situation was not more serious."

I glanced once more over at Brodie, that dark gaze unreadable. I took that as not a good sign. I could only imagine the tirade and lecture I would receive once Mr. Brimley was gone.

I should have been surprised when Brodie had returned quite urgently, the door thrown back against the far wall, and Mr. Brimley had followed shortly thereafter. I was not.

It took no deductive powers to know how he had learned of my encounter after Constable McLean contacted Inspector Dooley.

"You will be right as rain in no time," Mr. Brimley said as he stood and prepared to leave.

"Not nearly as serious as a bullet wound," he concluded. Then he issued instructions for Brodie. "Be certain to add more pieces of ice to that rubber pouch. It will help reduce the swelling. And take care, Miss Forsythe," he added, "not to encounter such situations if at all possible."

There had been no opportunity before Mr. Brimley's arrival to discuss the situation at the museum with Brodie. It might now serve as a diversion to avoid that lecture about being careful that I anticipated.

"The person who attacked me was obviously hiding in that stone casket," I commented, deliberately choosing not to wait for criticism or a lecture about being careful.

"It is possible they were there earlier on the day Sir Nelson was killed, and they possibly returned."

There was only silence as Brodie added more ice to the ingenious pouch Mr. Brimley had provided, made of India rubber, he had explained.

Brodie tied it off and crossed to where I sat and pulled up a chair opposite. Pinning me in so that there was no escape?

"And there are two items missing from the exhibit," I continued, in an attempt to appeal to his investigative nature.

And still silence, as he brushed my hair aside and gently pressed the pouch against the lump on the back of my head.

I frowned, not from the pain, of which there was still some, but from the silence.

I had learned how to navigate my way around the occasional arguments, his angry objections, and that stubborn Scots determination to protect me. For the most part. I was not accustomed to this.

"The inlaid box was there when we first saw the exhibit," I continued as he gently kneaded the tense muscles in the back of my neck.

"It's not there now, and someone went to considerable effort to hide the fact by moving the remaining four jars about."

He continued to hold that pouch filled with ice against the back of my head with one hand, while he continued to gently massage the back of my neck. It was quite wonderful. I gathered my thoughts once more.

"It doesn't make sense that someone would want to take jars containing two-thousand-year-old human organs," I suggested in an effort to draw him into conversation.

"And most fortunate that the hound was there, as you suggested," I continued. A compliment wouldn't hurt. Oh my, I thought, as he switched the pouch to his other hand and gently massaged the other side of my neck.

"It appears ..." I gathered my thoughts once more, "... that he attacked whoever was hiding in that casket. There is a piece of cloth in my bag covered in blood."

All my best efforts scattered as I slowly closed my eyes and simply gave in to that marvelous touch.

I have no idea how long we sat there with the quiet between us, and that soothing touch.

"Ye need to rest."

I slowly opened my eyes.

There was no lecture, not the usual tirade about 'taking myself off alone'—I had, after all, taken Rupert with me. Nor was there any anger.

For the first time since he had burst through the office door, looking very much like a crazy man, that dark gaze met mine as he pulled me to my feet.

"Ye will be the death of me."

Such kind words. If my head didn't feel as if it might explode, I would have said something. As it was, I would save it for later. It hurt to talk.

Brodie tucked me into the bed in the adjacent room.

"My notes ..." I protested.

"They will wait," he said as he bent over and kissed me on the forehead, then drew down the shade and doused the electric light.

Aggravating man, I thought, as I drifted off.

I was vaguely aware that he woke me at least twice during the night—according to Mr. Brimley's instructions—and in spite of my protests, provided me with something to drink, and tucked blankets around me once more.

It was early when I wakened, light barely visible at the edge of the window shade, the smell of coffee and voices, barely discernible, drifting beneath the closed door.

I slowly swung my legs over the edge of the bed. All things considered, I felt quite recovered, except for a dull ache at the back of my head.

Brodie had removed my long skirt and shirtwaist. Both lay over the chairback beside the bed.

His voice rose and sharpened. I quickly dressed, pulled on my boots, put some order to my hair, and stepped into the outer office.

Brodie was seated at the desk in a deceptively relaxed manner, leaning back in his chair, one arm resting casually on the desk.

I say *deceptively*, as that dark gaze met mine in silent warning. I had seen that look before when he was confronted by someone he either didn't trust or had a dislike for.

The man across from him, where I usually sat, was familiar. We had met previously. Mr. Brown qualified on both counts, someone Brodie disliked and didn't trust.

The man was as coarse looking as I remembered, from his shirt and trousers, to his grizzled beard, and his scarred bald head. And there was the faintly leering grin as he looked up from their conversation and that calculating gaze met mine.

"Mrs. Brodie is it now? And such lovely red hair and a comely figure." There was a look back at Brodie. "You are full of surprises, Brodie."

An insult and a compliment all in one. When I would have replied to that, I caught the not quite subtle shake of Brodie's head, and the equally not-subtle way his hand curled into a fist.

"As ye were saying, Mr. Brown ..."

"As I was saying," Brown continued as he turned and smiled at me. "You might want to make inquiries about several shipments by rail that have gone out from Portsmouth the past two years, apparently to the same location each time, I'm hearin', and right under the nose of the tax man," he added.

There was a subtle change in his manner, I thought. And perhaps out from under *his* nose as well?

"A trade ripe for the taking, to be certain."

"When was the last shipment?" Brodie inquired.

"More information? For that I might ask a favor from yerself," Brown replied as that smile deepened and he looked at me.

Brodie didn't so much as move, but it was there in the way his eyes narrowed. "There are some things that the price is more than ye would be willing to pay."

Rather than a threat, that sounded very much like a promise, I thought.

"I've no one I trust out of Portsmouth, but if you were to find some cargo there, I might take a small fee for telling you of it."

Brown stood to leave, that smile still on his face. "You remind me of myself, Mr. Brodie." He turned and made a mocking bow in my direction.

"And Mrs. Brodie. A pleasure, always."

As he turned to leave, the door opened, and I caught the

silhouette of a figure there, waiting. The door closed behind Mr. Brown and his equally imposing companion. And his comment to Brodie. That they were alike?

"And I thought before that the man could not be more disgusting."

I went to the door and opened it once more.

"Wot are ye doin'?"

"Mr. Brown has a particular odor about him." I didn't want to speculate on that. "Fresh air will help enormously."

"Is that right?" Brodie rose from behind his desk and crossed the office. He slipped his arms about me.

"How are ye this mornin', other than lookin' as if ye might want to remove the man's head?"

He did smell deliciously of cinnamon. I couldn't resist a taste.

"I'm hungry."

"Now I know of a certainty that ye will live," he replied.

We ate at the public house across the Strand. I ordered an extra breakfast for Mr. Cavendish, with sausages for Rupert.

"Do you believe Mr. Brown regarding those shipments?" I asked over more coffee while we waited for that extra breakfast.

"I believe he'd like to make a fee."

A thief stealing from thieves? Most interesting.

"If he doesn't know precisely where, how are we to learn where they might have gone?"

There *was* someone who might assist with that, if another shipment should arrive sent from there. Someone who had *perhaps* smuggled or stolen an object or two in the past.

I shouldn't have been surprised.

"Munro?"

"Let us just say, that he has some experience in such things."

The pot and the kettle?

That naturally raised the question, how much did my great aunt know about his other activities?

I remembered very clearly the night Munro and I had left Sussex Square under cover of darkness on another inquiry case, and had set off into a part of London that he seemed to know quite well, after leaving my great aunt's estate through what was called the smuggler's gate.

My first encounter with Mr. Brown. And while he had been most helpful at the time, I didn't trust the man. And I didn't like the smell of him either.

Once more I caught Brodie watching me, that earlier expression on his face—quiet, thoughtful, and I was fairly certain I knew what was there.

"I am quite all right," I assured him. "And you might tell me the reason Inspector Dooley was here last night. And quite late."

Rather than argue the point, Brodie shook his head.

"He brought word that Howard Carter has been released."

I was relieved. I had been concerned for him, yet after Mr. Hosni was found murdered and the attack on myself, it seemed for any logical thinking person that he could not possibly be the murderer, secured in the holding facility at Bow Street. However, we were talking *logical* thinking, which often seemed in short supply with the MET. Particularly regarding one C.I. Abberline, who was still on leave after questionable conduct in a previous case.

We returned to the office, and I made use of the accommodation room down the passageway for a rather hasty bath. I changed into other clothes that were there from a previous stay-over.

Afterward I sat at the desk across from Brodie and made notes from the previous day's encounter. I made my usual notes on the chalkboard, including that encounter with Mr. Brown.

"I want to return to the Exhibit Hall at the museum. There may be something more there, some clue that could be helpful. And I suppose we should go to Sussex Square so that you can speak with Munro."

"Do ye mean there might be somethin' that you overlooked or failed to see?" Brodie replied as he rose from behind the desk, went to the coat stand, and retrieved his jacket.

"Two pairs of eyes," I reminded him.

Eleven

MORE THAN ONCE ON the ride to the museum, I caught Brodie watching me with that expression I had seen the night before—thoughtful, with a frown before looking away.

"There is no need to worry," I assured him. "It was only a bump on the head."

"Aye," he replied. "I forgot how hard-headed ye can be."

Not unlike a stubborn Scot?

"The director and his staff may have already made their inspection ... however there are things that we might recognize that could provide a clue."

We entered through the main entrance and made our way to the Egyptian Exhibit Hall where a constable was positioned outside the entrance.

He greeted Brodie in that familiar way of those who had once worked with him while serving with the Metropolitan Police.

"I will need to let the director know that you are here," he informed us.

Sir Edward took my hand when he arrived. "I was most distressed after what happened yesterday. You have recovered?"

I thanked him for his concerns. He accompanied us into the exhibit hall.

"The situation has become most untenable. First Sir Nelson, then Mr. Hosni, this latest attack, and now ..." He was quite beside himself.

"You must come to my office afterward. There is something you must know."

It did seem that he was upset over something else. I assured him that we would.

I had brought the catalogue Mr. Hosni was working on. Once left to ourselves, as the constable was once more positioned outside the entrance, I went followed the steps of my visit the previous day.

"I started here and began verifying the artifacts against the information Mr. Hosni had made in his entries for the catalogue. It took some time, as they are listed separately. I started with the exhibits to the right. That forced me to look each one up separately."

It was quiet inside the exhibit hall, as to be expected with it closed to visitors. The only sounds were our footsteps as I slowly retraced mine with Brodie a few paces behind as he made his own observations.

When searching a place where a crime had taken place, I had learned that we each saw different things. As for myself, each step I took I looked at each individual artifact or those in cabinets as I had the day before. No small task, in consideration of the number of artifacts that were on display.

I eventually approached the part of the exhibit where the two caskets stood, along with the display of canopic jars that had once surrounded the gold-inlaid box. Brodie was there as I explained what I had found in the display.

"And the casket?"

It was the one nearest the display of jars.

I approached it as I had the day before. And, as the day before, pointed out the lid that had been moved back.

It was then I noticed something I hadn't noticed before when I was attacked—a familiar scent. The same scent Brodie had noticed in the police holding facility where Sir Nelson's body was taken—absinthe.

He approached the casket as well. We exchanged a look.

"It would seem there is the possibility that Sir Nelson's murderer made a return visit."

But what did that mean? That the murderer had a prefer-ence for that scent? The next question was—who? And if the person I had encountered had murdered Sir Nelson and Mr. Hosni, what was the reason?

The obvious answer seemed to be that, whoever it was, the person had a penchant for small carved figures or possibly petrified organs? It was a morbid thought.

Or was there some other reason?

Brodie turned on his hand-held light and shone it down through the opening into the casket.

"It's empty."

A casket with no mummified remains?

"And a convenient hiding place when ye returned unex-pectedly to verify the catalogue."

It wasn't that I doubted him, yet the description Mr. Hosni had written for those stone caskets had specifically mentioned that each contained mummified remains.

"That makes no sense," I replied as I peered down through the opening into the empty casket.

"The contents might have been taken before it arrived," Brodie suggested.

I supposed that might be possible. Or possibly after it arrived? That would explain someone being there when I returned the day before—someone I would like to return the favor to, after that blow to the head. I imagined someone fleeing across London, searching for some hiding place with a mummy. Not exactly something that would go unnoticed.

And the question, who would want to steal mummified remains?

I continued my search through the exhibit for anything else that might be missing.

However, it appeared that with the exception of that gold-handled knife Sir Nelson had been killed with and the painted box that was now missing, everything else was as it had been the day before and when Mr. Hosni had inspected the exhibit to verify it for the catalogue he was working on.

I paused before a display of weapons the Egyptians had used that had been among the artifacts discovered by Sir Nelson. I had not had the opportunity the day before to venture this far into the exhibit.

There were spears, shields, swords, bows, and a Khopesh. I had seen one before on my travel to Egypt.

It was a short, sickle-shaped sword. I imagined how one might wield it. The possibilities were quite dreadful. Had one been used to kill Mr. Hosni?

"Wot have ye found?" Brodie asked. "Is something else missing?"

"Not as far as I can tell. It's this sword. It's called a Khopesh, adapted from the ancient Greeks. For one who knew how to use it, it was supposedly a fearsome weapon."

My second tour of the exhibit brought me back around to that imposing statue of Ramses II.

"Yer thinkin' of the curse?" Brodie asked. "That makes two encounters," he reminded me.

"I don't believe in them." I thought of the amulet Mr. Hosni had given me. He obviously believed in such things, yet he had given it to me.

"Or someone wants ye to believe in it," he pointed out.

Which raised another question—perhaps to deter Brodie and me off the case? That raised another question. Who would have known that Mr. Hosni gave the amulet to me?

Satisfied that the other artifacts in the exhibit were undisturbed, Brodie and I signed out with the constable who had been placed on duty at the entrance to the exhibit hall.

We made our way to the director's office. He had seemed extremely upset when we first arrived.

"Come in, come in," he greeted us with that same sense of urgency and motioned for Brodie to close the door after.

"There has been a most disturbing development regarding the exhibit." Sir Edward paced the office. He picked up a piece of stationary from his desk and handed it to Brodie.

"A claim on the exhibit?" Brodie asked.

I had glimpsed the seal of the office of the French Ambassador as he read the official letter.

He nodded. "A letter regarding the exhibit has also been received from the French Foreign Secretary requesting that we release the artifacts to Dr. Duvalier."

"Edmund Duvalier?" I replied with more than a little surprise.

"Under the present circumstances," he continued, quite beside himself. "I have contacted the Home Secretary to request more time to respond so that you might be able to resolve this dreadful situation. This is a very delicate issue. I have patrons who supported the museum financially. Lady Antonia Montgomery is one of them. If they thought that the artifacts were stolen ..."

I saw his point. It could be devastating for the museum.

"There must have been paperwork that accompanied the artifacts," I commented.

"Yes, of course. Sir Nelson provided all the necessary paperwork from the Ministry of Antiquities in Cairo. Everything is in order."

Apparently not everything, if a claim was being made.

He shook his head. "There has never been anything like this before. I trusted Sir Nelson, and yet ... I don't understand how any of this has happened."

Now two people were dead, and there was a missing artifact, not to mention I had been attacked.

There was even more urgency to solve the case, with the rightful ownership of the Egyptian collection in question.

We left the museum and directed the driver to Sussex Square.

Brodie wanted to meet with Munro regarding the information Mr. Brown had given him.

Munro was manager of my great aunt's estates. He also oversaw all shipments of whisky that was distilled at Old Lodge in the north of Scotland. It appeared that he had connections into all sort of enterprises, much like Brodie.

Be that as it may, he had proven himself loyal to my great aunt and Lily on more than one occasion. And he had a keen mind for numbers, people, and how to deal with them.

My great aunt had rewarded him with the position of manager of her estates after he discovered her former manager stealing several cases of wine from her estate in France, that he then sold and made a substantial profit.

"You know the man, Duvalier?" Brodie asked as we left the museum.

"By reputation through Sir William Flinders-Petrie, and a chance encounter in Lisbon when I was there on travel. The man is quite despicable. He is French, however he owes no loyalty to any person, or country for that matter. He will sell his services to anyone."

"Ye have just described a thief."

It seems that I had. "He considers himself the ultimate authority on Egyptian antiquities ... and women," I added.

"Ye had an experience with the man?"

"I will only say that he ended up on his backside."

"Taking liberties, was he?"

I could have sworn he found it all quite amusing.

"My other choice was to use the knife Munro had me carry when I traveled. However, I did not want to stain my gown."

"So, the man has a reputation for being a thief, a womanizer, and owes loyalty to no one but himself. Ye have described the perfect criminal."

And now he had managed to persuade the French Ambassador to lay claim to the artifacts in the Egyptian Museum. No doubt, for a fee.

The traffic across the city was congested, and I thought of the underground rail system that the city had planned. There were already short-run rail connections between a half dozen rail stations, but expansion had been delayed by rivalries.

I had read what was being called a 'tube railway network' was not practical until electric power was available throughout. And there were the usual financial difficulties with cautious investors. It would be quite marvelous, *if* it actually came about.

Aunt Antonia was in the game room with Lily in a most serious game of billiards when we arrived. A quick study no matter what she took on, Lily had apparently won the last game. And possibly more.

My great aunt looked up as we arrived. "She's won another round," she said with some pique.

"I'm a bit off my game. It is undoubtedly due to a sore muscle in my shoulder."

Undoubtedly, I thought as I noticed Brodie's amused expression. She handed me her stick.

"How are you, my dear?" she asked. I exchanged a glance with Brodie. How was it possible that she knew about the incident the day before?

"You are quite well, it seems. I refuse to worry, and now that you're here, you can play the next game."

Lily had what could only be described as a devious grin.

"Her Ladyship told me that ye beat Mr. Munro two rounds out of three," she said with a sly smile. "I beat him the last time."

That did sound like a challenge. How could I possibly resist, even though it had been some time since I last picked up a stick?

"Prepare to lose, young lady," I told her, taking off my jacket and laying it over a nearby chair as Brodie inquired where he might find Munro.

"He was off to the stables, the last I spoke with him," my great aunt replied. "You must join me for a bit of refreshment. I do believe Mikaela and Lily will be at it for some time."

Unless I was mistaken, 'refreshment' referred to a bit of Old Lodge single malt whisky.

BRODIE

Munro was in the stables that also contained Lady Antonia's motor carriage.

'A dangerous development,' Mikaela called it. Not necessarily for her great aunt, but anyone who happened to get in her way when she decided to take herself off on an excursion.

Much like someone else he knew.

"Smuggling?" Munro replied when he had explained the case he and Mikaela had taken after Sir Nelson's murder. And shared the information Otis Brown had given them.

His friend spat on the ground when Brodie mentioned he had spoken with Brown.

"Ye know well enough the man canna be trusted. He's no better than the ones yer lookin' for, might even be part of it."

Brodie had thought about that, an 'arrangement' that Brown and his people had been cheated out of, and the possibility that he and Mikaela were being used to find the ones Brown was also looking for.

"He claims there are goods out of Portsmouth that have been directed to other places."

"Ye want to send someone to verify shipments."

"Not just 'someone,'" Brodie clarified.

Munro nodded. "It would be faster to go there by rail, faster still if there were two to make inquiries."

Brodie agreed. "Two days with travel would be sufficient. If ye can arrange it."

"I can. What about the stolen artifacts?"

"It seems a claim has been made on them through the

French ambassador. Mikaela will make inquiries through people she knows in that regard."

"And a way to keep her here in London?"

Brodie nodded.

"Yer playin' a dangerous game if she learns of it."

She did have a fierce temper. He would cross that bridge if it happened.

They agreed to meet at the rail station for the early train south from London in the morning."

"Bring yer work clothes," Brodie added. "We dinna want to raise suspicion from those we encounter."

The arrangements made, he returned to the parlor adjacent to the gaming room.

"Most refreshing," Lady Antonia announced as he poured her another dram, since the first one was quickly consumed.

They sat together before the fire that one of the servants had lit in the fireplace against a chill that had set in as they watched the billiards game.

"You've spoken with Mr. Munro?"

"Aye."

She followed the direction of his gaze on the game that was in progress in the adjacent room and noticed the frown.

"Regarding the man Hosni's murder at the museum, I presume. And now the encounter Mikaela had at the museum. Such a tragic affair."

Details of the second murder had not been put out on the street or in the dailies.

"Ye seem to be well informed."

She waved off his surprise. "You are not the only one who

has their sources, Mr. Brodie. Mine are usually quite reliable." She raised her glass in a toast and smiled again.

"You should know that I have dismissed Lily's latest tutor," she said. "Or rather he tendered his resignation. It seems there is nothing more that he can teach her. She has excelled at her letters and numbers.

"Of course, her climbing out the second-story window after declaring herself quite through, may have had something to do with it," she added, quite amused.

"Much like another?" Brodie commented. He had heard of some of Mikaela's exploits at very near the same age.

"And myself perhaps," she confessed.

He frowned.

"There does seem to be concern there regarding Lily," she keenly observed as she watched him.

"And do not look at me that way, Mr. Brodie," she admonished him. "I do know my way around the male of the species. I should at my age, and I suppose marriage can be a devilish proposition. Most fortunate that she had Rupert with her or the situation might have ended differently," she added.

"It is only natural for you to be concerned for her." She was certain she had struck upon his concern.

"An unusual relationship to be certain," she commented, then smiled at the memory.

"There was a man when I was quite young. He was not acceptable, as far as my father was concerned. He wanted someone more ... *appropriate* for someone of my station. Not to mention the scandal it would have caused." She brushed that off.

"Particularly considering the man's ... vocation."

"I canna imagine," Brodie commented. Her smile deepened.

"It was the fire, and oh how we burned." She angled a look over at him. "I do believe, Mr. Brodie, that we must seize the fire from time to time, even if it means we may get burned."

She held out her glass for another dram.

"And I assure you, all these years later, if I had it to do all over again, I would not choose otherwise."

She smiled as he poured her glass. "You cannot change her. Therefore, the question you must ask yourself, can you live without her? If not, you must accept what you cannot change." She lifted her glass in a toast.

"Pour yourself another and enjoy the fire."

MIKAELA

I won the third game and declined 'just one more' at Lily's protest.

"Ye have to let me have a chance to beat ye," she replied, obviously disappointed.

Aunt Antonia had invited us to remain for supper; however, I wanted to return to the office on the Strand to make my latest notes in our inquiry case that had taken yet another turn.

Two people were dead, I had been attacked by someone who managed to hide himself in the exhibit, and an artifact was now missing.

Howard Carter had originally been detained under suspicion, since he was the last to see Sir Nelson alive. However, it was obvious that he could not have killed Mr. Hosni while detained at the Yard. Unless, of course, he was a magician who performed a disappearing act, which he was not.

We had discovered that there was a great deal of enmity on the part of Sir Nelson's nephew, who was not the least distraught over his uncle's death. There was a curse to deal with, and now a claim by the French government that the artifacts belonged to them.

Not to mention that unusual scent of absinthe that had been present upon the examination of Sir Nelson's body, and then again when Brodie and I returned to the museum after my encounter with whoever was in that casket—most certainly not a mummified body.

Taken altogether, there was potential motive from the French, opportunity aplenty, and the means was quite obvious as well in someone who had a penchant for knives and ancient swords.

Brodie sat across from me in the coach as we returned across London to the office on the Strand, that dark gaze watching me.

"It's been a long day. How are ye?"

I confessed to a bit of a headache.

"I'll be going to Portsmouth with Munro on the morning train to make inquiries about any unusual shipments. "While ye make yer inquiries with the French Ambassador, since ye have met the man.

"He might be more forthcoming with ye, considerin' yer family connections. And a seaport is no place for a woman. It might raise suspicion over the information we'll be trying to learn. Two pair of hands, as ye like to tell me. Or three in this case."

I knew what he was doing. He was using my words against me to persuade me that it was better that I remain in London. I reminded myself that he could be such a devil.

Nevertheless, as much as I hated to admit the logic of it, even if it was a bit underhanded, he was right that the French Ambassador might very well be more likely to speak with me about the claim that was being made on the artifacts in the exhibit.

"Of course, dear."

We traveled the rest of the way back to the Strand in silence except for the occasional creak of the coach or when Mr. Hastings called out to the team.

"Good evenin', miss." Mr. Cavendish greeted me when we arrived. He inquired about my encounter the day before.

I assured him that I was quite all right.

"The hound is no worse for it," he commented. "He'd like to have another go at the man who attacked you."

I, for one, hoped there would not be another encounter such as that one. I inquired if supper was still being served at the Public House in spite of the late hour.

He grinned up at me. "Chicken pie is on the menu. It's a favorite with those after they leave work for the day. The hound and I will see what is left."

Brodie followed me up the stairs.

I had removed my jacket and hung it on the coat stand, then retrieved my notebook and went to the chalkboard to make my notes there while we waited for supper to arrive.

I heard the usual sounds as Brodie moved about the office. He hung his coat on the coat stand, went to the desk, and removed the revolver he usually carried and slipped it into the drawer.

He stoked up the fire in the fire box, and crossed to the side table. There was the distinctive clink of glass. Then he was there, and handed me one of the tumblers with a dram of my great aunt's very fine whisky.

I had added Edmund Duvalier's name to the list of those who were connected to the artifacts, or at least claimed to be.

"Ye do not like the man," Brodie commented.

I took a sip of whisky.

"He not an explorer. He has more the reputation of a broker in antiquities, to the highest bidder. In this case that would seem to be the French government."

"Yer not certain?"

"I learned from Sir Nelson that there are those who will go to any length to possess what they want, if they have enough money."

"Aye, collectors with too much money," he added. "When it could be used to help others."

I nodded.

"A man like that could be dangerous," he commented.

"He's more like an irritating insect. Somehow I don't see him as a murderer."

"Your conversation with Aunt Antonia seemed quite serious," I commented.

He took the glass from my hand and set it on the table.

"She reminded me that I canna change ye."

"Did she now? The pot calling the kettle black? She is not without her adventures."

"Ay, she told me. The devil of it is, that I love ye," he said.

He had told me before that I was important to him, at Old Lodge when he asked me to marry him. But he had never said those three words. He was not a man who spoke of his feelings, and I could only imagine what it took for him to say it now.

He slipped his hands back through my hair, and leaned his forehead against mine. "And when I saw ye yesterday afterward ..." He had gone quiet for a moment.

"She said that I have a choice, since I canna change ye." He kissed me.

"I'll take the fire," he whispered against my lips as the pins in my hair scattered to the floor.

Twelve

BRODIE LEFT EARLY from the office to meet Munro at the rail station that was to take them to Portsmouth. He had dressed the part of the common worker so as not to draw undue attention. Portsmouth was a place Munro knew well from overseeing shipments from France for my great aunt.

It was hoped they might be able to learn something about stolen artifacts. As Munro explained it, everything that went dockside in a port was well-known, legitimate or otherwise, in that way of gossip or rumor.

It was the work that went on 'otherwise' —in other words, smuggling—that he and Brodie were most interested in, as well as the connections for those shipments.

There were many people who thought smuggling had long been eliminated, with the Royal Coast Guard keeping watch over everything that arrived at British ports. Munro had merely laughed when I mentioned it at the time.

"It's verra much alive and well, and very lucrative."

I didn't ask if it was dangerous, that went without saying, and Brodie left well-armed. Still ...

After he left, I placed a telephone call to my great aunt. She was well acquainted with the Home Secretary, I had learned from a previous case.

"Of course, dear," she had replied. *"Just give me a little time to put myself together and I will make a telephone call to Sir Henry. A meeting with the French Ambassador, you say? That would be Sir Thomas Waddington. Don't let the title fool you, he is not a gentleman."* she added with noticeable disdain.

"You might want to make certain that you have that weapon Mr. Munro gave you."

As for the Home Secretary, Sir Henry Matthews was a 'very dear old friend.'

I did wonder from time to time about all those who were well-placed whom she knew, or had some influence with. It was undoubtedly one of those things best not to know.

Brodie had once exclaimed with surprise at someone else she was well-acquainted with.

"Is there anyone she doesna know? The Queen perhaps?"

I had informed him she was also well-acquainted with the Queen and the Prince of Wales. That had brought one of those typically Scottish sounds.

"And I suppose ye know them as well?"

Not all of them, I admitted at the time.

Aunt Antonia promised to return my telephone call at the town house once she was able to speak with *'dear Henry,'* after admitting that the telephone was most convenient for such things.

"Stolen artifacts …" she exclaimed. *"This is exciting."*

That little voice inside me warned that I probably needed to have a conversation with her. This did not mean she was part of our investigation—she was merely providing information.

That could be a delicate matter, however, as she had

mentioned how thrilling it was to assist us before. That conversation had included 'how exciting it all was, and crime was so fascinating.'

Fascinating and exciting were not exactly how I would have described murder, being shot, or chasing down those who had taken my sister captive. It was often frustrating and terrifying.

After she assured me that she would prevail, I packed the bag I usually carried when on a case, locked the office, and returned to Mayfair.

I had no sooner stepped through the doorway than Mrs. Ryan informed me that my great aunt had called.

As much as I appreciated her assistance, not to mention her connections to the Home Secretary, the excitement she had conveyed to Mrs. Ryan did not bode well.

I had returned her call and she informed me that '*dear Henry*' had arranged an appointment for me with the French Ambassador that afternoon.

"*Do remember to be careful around Sir Thomas Waddington,*" she had cautioned. "*The man has a way with the ladies, but he really is such a toad. Although, should he attempt to take advantage an encounter with Mr. Brodie would be most interesting.*"

I chose my clothes for the meeting with the French Ambassador as I would a business meeting with my publisher or banker, and wore my hair up. Heeding my great aunt's warning, I tucked the knife Munro had given me inside of my right boot.

I occupied myself at my writing desk as I made entries regarding Brodie's travel to Portsmouth, and my pending appointment with the French Ambassador.

The driver Mrs. Ryan had called for arrived in good time. I slipped my notebook with questions I had regarding

Monsieur Duvalier and supposed 'rumors' of stolen artifacts into my bag, then set off for my appointment with Sir Thomas.

The French Embassy where he had an office was very near Knightsbridge at the entrance to Hyde Park. The flag of the French Republic waved from atop the white brick building with that entrance framed by four columns.

I was shown to the desk of the under-secretary to the Ambassador, who went to the office of Sir Thomas to announce my arrival.

I was forced to wait as I was informed that he was presently engaged in another appointment, the young man with a poor attempt at a mustache, who was the under-secretary, informed me with a hint of disdain as he spoke in French. He turned to leave.

I responded in fluent French from my school days and informed him that I did have another appointment pending— not precisely the truth, yet it did encourage him to return to the Ambassador's office ten minutes later to inquire if he would be longer.

Arrogant, pompous young man, I thought, and he couldn't even grow a decent mustache. I kept my smile to myself as Sir Thomas's 'previous appointment' exited quite shortly, nodded to me, then left. I was promptly escorted into his office.

He rose from behind his desk in greeting, speaking in perfect English as the under-secretary. I did have a devilish thought about that title, *under-secretary*. Something along the line of what particular rock had the young man crawled out from *under*, as I turned to the ambassador in greeting.

He was a short, portly man with a bush of side whiskers that I thought always seemed to be in need of a trim on most men, thinning gray hair that he smoothed back, and beady little eyes.

My great aunt had a thought about beady eyes, something she had commented on years before. A warning actually, as she accompanied my sister and me to Paris at the beginning of our school years there.

"Never trust a man with beady eyes. They are usually contemplating some mischief. Devious creatures, and they will lie to you."

I had no idea the reason she singled me out for that bit of wisdom. Well, actually I did. And she had been proven correct on more than one occasion.

He was cordial as I entered his office.

"I have not previously had the pleasure, Lady Forsythe. The Home Secretary did say you needed to speak to me about a matter most urgent."

I briefly explained the two deaths at the museum, along with the artifact that had apparently been stolen.

"Most terrible. Sir Henry did explain this to me and asked that I provide whatever assistance in finding those responsible."

I inquired about rumors of artifacts being smuggled into the country by those less scrupulous, most particularly Edmund Duvalier. He pretended to know nothing of the man.

"It is well known by certain individuals that he arranged for a shipment in the past year that included a sarcophagus, as well as several extremely valuable funerary pieces for one of the auction houses," I reminded him of what we had learned from Mr. Brown.

"It seems that he is well-connected, perhaps with more than one wealthy buyer." I took a chance on the next bit of information. "It is said that one of his clients is French. And now apparently, your government is making claims on the exhibit at the museum.

"It would seem that you could hardly *not* know of the man. In view of the recent murders, it might very well go a long way to clearing your government of any connection to these illegal activities."

He left his chair and rounded the desk.

"I have heard of Monsieur Duvalier's activities," he said in a patronizing voice. "And my government would never condone such heinous activities as murder, my dear lady."

I cringed at his boldness. Not precisely an answer. I wanted information.

"It would go a long way to reassuring the Home Secretary that your government is not involved in this in any way, if you were able to provide information as to where Monsieur Duvalier might be found." I pointed out.

"You are such an intriguing woman, Lady Forsythe. Such things are usually left to the inquiries of men."

I simply smiled.

"Of course, I will see what information we have regarding Monsieur Duvalier."

With that he crossed the office, summoned the under-secretary, and made the request in a rapid dialogue of his own language, for his 'meddling guest' to make certain no difficulties arose with the English.

I caught the alarmed expression at the under-secretary's face after our previous exchange in their language. He mumbled a response, and the door was closed before he could inform the Ambassador.

"It will be done, Lady Forsythe. Before you leave, we will have the information and provide it to you."

I rose from my chair and thanked him. From the notes I'd

made, I was fairly certain, as was Brodie, that Duvalier was key to this. Now, I intended to find out for certain.

As I turned to leave, the ambassador was there, not exactly blocking me but very insistent as he ran his fingers up my arm, his intentions obvious.

"You may require more information, Lady Forsythe. Perhaps over luncheon, or a late supper."

I was not naïve or inexperienced to such invitations. One could not travel to foreign countries, or even about in some of the places I had found myself in London since my first inquiry case with Brodie, and not encounter such propositions.

There was always some man who thought he could … *impose* himself on a woman. I was not one of those women.

"My husband seems to think there are those who would attempt to take advantage." I explained.

"I have assured him that he need not be concerned."

Those beady eyes gleamed.

"I always carry a revolver when I am out and about. One can never be too careful. Wouldn't you agree, monsieur?"

"You are right, of course, Lady Forsythe. I must prepare for my next appointment, if you will excuse me."

I smiled to myself—that did seem rather abrupt.

He opened the door and hastily reminded the under-secretary of the information I had requested.

The young man nodded and handed him a note card with information printed on the reverse side for his inspection. Sir Thomas Waddington made a somewhat hasty gesture.

"I am certain that the information is correct." He handed me the note card and hastily bid me good day.

I thanked the under-secretary and followed him to the front entrance of the embassy building, and found a carriage nearby.

Now, to see if there was any word from Brodie or Munro.

It was very near midday when I returned to the office on the Strand, and Mr. Cavendish informed me there were no messages.

He was familiar with most areas of London, for reasons there was no need for me to know. He was a very clever fellow when it came to providing information from time to time.

The information I had received included that the last known place of residence for Monsieur Duvalier was in the company of an actress by the name of Sophie Marquette.

While my acquaintance with my good friend Templeton introduced me to others in her chosen profession from time to time, I was not familiar with a woman by that name.

However, Templeton might be some help there. It was apparent that Monsieur Duvalier did not keep his own residence, for obvious reasons.

Nor was there any message from Brodie or Munro, Mr. Cavendish informed me. Not unusual, I told myself, as I climbed the stairs to the second-floor landing and let myself into the office.

I placed a telephone call to my great aunt and thanked her for assisting with the Home Secretary, and turned down an invitation for supper.

I let Rupert in when he appeared most insistently at the door, then placed a call to the Theatre Royal Drury Lane in an attempt to reach Templeton. I was informed that she had not yet arrived for the afternoon.

I occupied myself the next several hours making entries in my notebook and at the chalkboard, should Brodie and Munro return while I was out and about on some errand.

I was finally able to reach Templeton at the theatre. She insisted that I meet her. She had the most exciting news to tell me about her next tour, and it gave me the opportunity to find out what she knew about Sophie Marquette …

My friend had established a remarkable career for herself, I thought, as I arrived at the theatre and paid the cabman.

In the past, Templeton had toured the Continent, which included engagements in France, Spain, and Portugal, along with a brief engagement in Brazil, where she acquired Ziggy, her four-foot-long pet iguana.

Ziggy had spent a great deal of time terrorizing the audience of the theater where Templeton had performed at the time. He had eventually been sent to her country estate outside London, where he dined on roses—an enormous enclosed solarium full of them.

Templeton had also toured the United States and declared it her favorite, exclaiming that I really must consider going there. She had gone on and on about the sophistication of New York compared to the dangerous and exciting parts of the West.

In the past year, she had considered stepping away from the theatre after her current engagement at the Drury, to pursue other interests. After all, she was two years older than me, and she had to think about the future.

I did wonder whom that future might include, as she had carried on a colorful relationship with Munro for a while.

Yet, it seemed anything permanent between them was not to be, and now a new engagement had set her plans for retirement back, at least for the next year.

As I stepped through the entrance and told the attendant that Templeton was expecting me, I passed by that imposing statue of Sir William Shakespeare inside the grand foyer.

Templeton claimed to have some sort of psychic connection with his spirit. I did not necessarily believe in such things, yet there had been instances in the past when information she claimed had come from him had helped in our inquiry cases.

Coincidence? Something we would have learned in due time?

Perhaps, but I had learned from my travels and experiencing other cultures not to judge another for their beliefs.

And then there was that feeling that I'd had before, and again now, as I passed Sir William's statue and his gaze seemed to follow me, that there might be something to it. Brodie, of course, would have denied all of it. And that, of course, included ancient Egyptian curses.

I found my friend in full stage makeup and costume, preparing for her evening performance.

"I'm to go back to the United States! We're doing Richard III," she excitedly told me as we sat in her dressing room.

"New York, Boston, Chicago, Denver, with several places in between, and ending with a full month in San Francisco! It's a minor part, Queen Margaret. But I have several important scenes. Sir William has said that I will do quite well with it."

There it was, William Shakespeare. She asked me about Brodie, which was her way of eventually asking about Munro. It did seem that there was still some interest there. I told her they were both off in the matter of our current inquiry case, which gave me the perfect opportunity to inquire about Sophie Marquette.

"She had a brief engagement at the Adelphi, but then missed several performances. I do seem to remember that she was having an affair with someone, and that may have been the cause."

I asked if the name Duvalier was familiar, according to the information the French Ambassador had given me.

"The man was English, well-placed and educated, from

what I heard," Templeton said. "He arranged for her to stay in the country when there was some difficulty about it. I heard a few weeks ago that she left—the gossip here and about."

"Do you know where she lived while she was here?"

She shook her head. "With her at the Adelphi, it could be one of the rooms let for performers nearby, since she stayed only a short time."

It was more than I had when I arrived. There were only one or two places where rooms were let for actors when in London. It would take some time, but it might provide important information. It was remotely possible if I could find Sophie Marquette, I might also find Duvalier.

And then there were the inevitable questions about Munro that eventually came round to my friend inquiring if there was any woman he was presently with. I had no way of knowing, and told her that. He didn't share that sort of information. Or with Brodie, for that matter, for which I was grateful.

"I'll be gone on tour for several months, and it might be good to see him again before I leave," she commented. "You know, something casual. Luncheon perhaps. Old friends?"

I thought of that mural Brodie and I had discovered in her private bedchamber at her country home during a previous case. Most colorful, and revealing. Luncheon perhaps? Casual?

And pigs fly ...

Thirteen

PORTSMOUTH

BRODIE

THEY TOOK the train from Waterloo Station. The third-class carriage was filled with workers dressed as they were, who kept to themselves; a family on holiday; two older women, sisters by the conversation he overheard; and others who couldn't afford the more expensive fares in the second-class carriage.

With three changeovers on the Southsea line, the trip was slow, rumbling into each station, passengers leaving as others climbed aboard. They eventually arrived in Portsmouth just after midday.

The Southsea line connected from Portsmouth Station to Portsmouth Harbor by tram, and included the line to Brighton that he had taken over two years earlier at the end of another case.

Beyond the harbor was the Royal Naval shipyards and the ferry port, along with a sprawling city of government buildings, shops, street markets, and other businesses that spread in the distance to fields and farmlands.

Ferries ran between the harbor and the Isle of Wight, where the Queen took summer vacations with the royal family. But the Isle of Wight was not their destination.

Munro knew Portsmouth well from past trips for Mikaela's great aunt, along with places where they might find information.

"The docks, where other ships from across the channel put in, are down the way," he explained. "Along with taverns and stay-overs for the crews," Munro added as they boarded a horse-drawn tram.

"There is a man there who runs the private docks by the name of Campbell. I've worked with him before. He'll be able to tell us if Mr. Brown has sent us on a fool's errand."

The commercial docks swarmed with a congestion of warehouses, wagons and carts, draymen and dockworkers, public houses, taverns, with 'other' business establishments for those who put into port.

It was an organized chaos of shouting, cursing stevedores and longshoremen, arguments that broke out in a mix of languages, with drivers eager to be away with their loaded wagons on the last run of the day, before returning in the morning and starting all over again.

They passed the shipping office with an overhead board with the names of the four ships that were due in—two from LeHavre, one due from Calais, and a fourth due to arrive from Lisbon.

"Most of the dockworkers are part of organized labor," Munro explained. "Campbell works for the private warehouse owners and runs crews of workers for the day at a lower cost from private docks down the way."

They made their way past the shipping office, past wagons that were being loaded, through pallets stacked with hogsheads, barrels, and crates. Then they stepped into a warehouse with signage overhead—South Port Shipping Company.

Munro spoke briefly with a worker and was told that Campbell was up in the office at the back of the warehouse.

They slowly made their way through the maze of cargo on the floor of the warehouse.

Campbell was a large man with ham-like arms that suggested he might have worked the docks himself, unloading cargo ships. He had sharp eyes that narrowed when he recognized Munro.

"I've no cargo comin' in for you. What brings you to the south port, Mr. Munro? A special shipment perhaps? If so, the harbor will be full through well into tomorrow. However, for a fee, I could make a change if there is a ship comin' across."

Brodie listened to what was undoubtedly the usual conversation between his friend and the manager of this part of the docks.

"Not a cargo, but a bit of yer time, and some information," Munro replied.

"If her ladyship wasn't such a good customer, I would have yer worthless hide tossed out." Campbell motioned for Munro to close the door.

"Since I know you like to keep our conversations private," he added. "And you might introduce me to this man, so that I know exactly who I am dealing with."

Once introductions were made, Campbell sat back in his chair. "Portsmouth is far from London. And you say it's not about business for her ladyship. What might be the information you're looking for?"

Munro explained how the information had come to them.

"Mr. Brown?" It was followed by a curse, then a laugh. "The man is a thief and a cutthroat. I canna imagine doing business with him."

"He has provided 'information' in the past that has been reliable. And he owes me a favor," Brodie explained.

"Must be a large favor. But you don't trust the man or you wouldn't be here."

"It's in the matter of two murders," Brodie informed him. He had his full attention now.

"Are you with the bloody peelers?"

"It's a private inquiry case, and it may be connected to illegal shipments that Mr. Brown seemed to think might come through here," Munro replied.

"You know well enough, Mr. Munro, how hard it is to get any illegal cargo past the Royal Navy," Campbell pointed out.

Yet Brodie saw the interest that gleamed in that sharp gaze.

"Unless, of course, there's enough compensation in it."

There was a long silence.

"A man in my position, comes across a lot of information. You learn what might or might not be true, and it's always wise to be mindful of who can be trusted and who cannot."

There was more silence as they continued to wait. Campbell seemed to come to a decision.

"I've had to trust Mr. Munro here, more than once. He's never done me false. There is a man who occasionally finds himself with some items that a customer would prefer to keep from being noticed by the local authorities," he continued. "Those being the harbor patrols and the bloody Royal Navy.

"I could put the word out for him, if he would be willing to meet with you."

"When?" Brodie asked.

"That would depend on that fee we were discussing."

"We'd be fools fer certain to go about with substantial coin in our pockets," Munro pointed out.

"True enough," Campbell conceded. "But perhaps an arrangement for a portion of that next cargo of wine from France?" he suggested.

Munro shook his head. "That is no bargain. I'll not go against one who has treated me fair and true."

Campbell smiled. "Sit back down, my friend. We may still be able to strike a bargain." He turned to Brodie.

"What about you?" he asked. "A quiet man who says little and keeps to himself is dangerous, to my way of thinking, but ye may have a thought on the matter."

He had been watching Campbell. Men like him respected one thing—power, be it over the men who depended on him for their next meal, or those who relied on goods that entered port with shipping labels on crates that had been altered to disguise the contents—expensive and very lucrative contents that the authorities would be pleased to know about.

Brodie had no doubt that Campbell could be a dangerous man, and it was a dangerous game they played. He stood and crossed over to the windows that looked down on the warehouse floor below and the mountain of crates and other shipping containers secured in the warehouse until they could be sent off to customers.

Quid pro quo.

"There must have been a bit of a storm crossing the channel with the cargo below," he commented.

"Some broken merchandise perhaps in a crate labeled as ... cotton? It will be most interestin' if the millworkers waitin' to receive the shipment have a taste for brandy."

Silence filled the office. Brodie eventually turned from that window, his hand resting just inside the front of his jacket as he met that narrowed gaze.

"A bit of information for information kept to ourselves," Brodie told him.

Campbell slowly sat forward at the desk, that gaze locked on him. He made no effort to deny what Brodie had discovered in a puddle on the floor of the warehouse as they passed through, and suspected might be in those other crates.

"That cargo is worth several thousand pounds. You are either a brave man, or a fool."

"I suppose we shall find out which it is," Brodie replied. "Several thousand pounds of cargo safe in yer warehouse with none the wiser for it, in exchange for a conversation with that other person ye know."

Like Munro he trusted the man only as far as he could throw him, and for a man that size, that wasn't far.

"Ye may leave a message at the Blue Dolphin Inn," Munro told him. "We'll be expecting it."

"The Blue Dolphin?" Brodie inquired as they left the warehouse with a careful eye to their backs.

"It's the place I usually stay when I'm here on business for her ladyship, and Campbell knows it well enough," Munro replied as they reached the wharf. "But not tonight."

They took a late supper at a public house on the quay, then made their way back to the Blue Dolphin afterward.

A woman by the name of Molly greeted Munro as they entered the foyer where rooms were let for the night.

"I was wondering when you might come back this evenin'," she commented as her gaze slid past to Brodie. She smiled, the sort of smile that was an invitation.

"And you've brought a friend." She rounded the counter and approached Brodie.

"I've not seen you before." She reached out a hand and laid it against the front of his jacket, then moved lower.

Brodie stopped her with a hand at her wrist.

"Ah, Molly girl, ye best take care," Munro cautioned. "That one is marrit."

"A good many are," she replied with a slow smile. "It don't make no difference to me, or them."

"But this particular lady is a good shot and not bad with the blade either," Munro told her. "I taught her meself."

There was a frown that turned into a pout on the woman's face.

"I'd like to meet a 'lady' like that."

"No, ye would not," Munro told her.

Brodie firmly moved her hand away.

"Do ye perhaps have a message?" he asked.

She nodded. "I was holding it till ye came round for your usual room," she replied with a look at Munro.

"Perhaps later," he told her as she returned behind the front counter and retrieved the message.

"More's the pity for me," she said as she handed Munro the message.

He passed her a coin, and they left the Blue Dolphin.

The man's name was Davidson—Captain Davidson. According to the note, he could be found at the Bell and Anchor.

"Ye know the man?" Brodie asked.

"Know of."

"Smuggling?"

"Let us just say that he has a certain reputation around the docks."

"And bold enough to put into port right under the noses of the Royal Navy?" That told Brodie a lot about the man.

"Do ye know the Bell and Anchor?" he added

Munro nodded. "Aye, it's on the High Street. Those like this man will expect something in return if he has information on Duvalier."

"I've some coin with me," Brodie replied.

Not unlike London Docks, the inns and taverns in this part of Portsmouth worked a lively business and were open for that business in spite of the late hour of the night.

They had both been in such places and kept a watchful eye as they entered the tavern, where cigarette smoke hung in the air thick with the smell of ale. And there was that other smell of those who had perhaps been at sea for a good number of weeks, or perhaps months.

It was not difficult to know which man was Davidson. He sat at a table in the corner of the tavern with two other men who had the look of seamen, along with two women, the night's entertainment.

"Do ye have a plan?" Munro asked as they slowly made their way across the crowded tavern.

"See what the man knows, and not get ourselves killed," Brodie replied.

"Aye."

Davidson looked up as they approached the table. When Munro would have made introductions, he waved him off.

"I know who ye are," he told Munro. "Ye do business in Portsmouth from time to time." He looked at Brodie.

"We have not met."

Brodie introduced himself.

There was a slow nod. "Can I stand ye a drink?" Davidson asked.

"I'll stand *ye* one," Brodie replied. "For some information."

"Yer a Scot, right enough," Davidson commented. "Cautious but willing to do business."

"Aye."

Davidson nodded. "Have a seat and we'll talk."

Only when the drinks arrived, did he and Munro each take a chair at the table.

"And ye take care to sit with yer back to the wall," Davidson noted. "Ye've had some experience with that."

"Some," Brodie replied. He placed a gold sovereign on the table.

A second round eventually appeared and Brodie placed another sovereign on the table.

"A man who carries gold about in a place like this is either a brave man, or a fool," Davidson commented.

"There is more, for information that might be useful," Brodie told him.

There was another round and Davidson sat back in his chair. He seemed to have made a decision.

"Wot information might that be?"

Brodie wasn't fooled that the man trusted them, yet Munro's reputation went a long way toward that. At least they hadn't been outright refused.

And the gold sovereigns at the center of the table went even further for a man who apparently made his profit any way he could—legal or otherwise.

"We're looking for a man by the name of Duvalier who receives cargo from time to time for interested persons."

Davidson shrugged. "Wot sort of cargo?"

This was where everything could end. Davidson might know nothing about Duvalier. Or he might have carried cargo for Duvalier and would not risk jeopardizing his own 'business dealings.'

They were among thieves here. The question was, which among them might be willing to provide information, and at what price?

"Artifacts smuggled out of Egypt," Brodie replied. "For a private customer."

Davidson listened with an expression that revealed nothing.

"Ye workin' for the bloody British government?"

Brodie shook his head. "I've no interest in it. And if ye know Munro, ye already know he's not the sort to work for them. It's in the matter of two murders."

There was another shrug. "The risk of doing business," Davidson replied. "And now ye come to me?"

"Ye might know where Duvalier can be found."

There was a long silence. Davidson shrugged.

"One hears of such people."

And perhaps had even carried cargo illegal for him? Brodie speculated.

"Wot are ye proposing?" Davidson commented over yet another drink.

"A business transaction," Brodie replied and placed another gold sovereign on the table.

"Ye play a dangerous game, Mr. Brodie. Particularly in a place like this, with a good amount of gold coins on the table."

"There might be somethin' more to be had for ye, for the information," Munro told him.

Brodie angled his friend a sharp look. They hadn't spoken of more that he'd be willing to give the man for information.

"What might that be?" Davidson asked, obviously interested.

"An arrangement," Munro replied. "For cargo that is lucrative and for a percentage of each shipment."

"Wot are ye suggestin'?"

"A mutual agreement that could be verra lucrative for both my employer and yerself, in exchange for the information that could help find the murderer."

"A business arrangement?"

"There's been some difficulty from time to time," Munro explained without going into details. "If an arrangement could be made, it would also include certain shipments coming back from France."

Brodie knew they were discussing shipments of Old Lodge whisky and wine shipments to England from Lady Montgomery's properties in the south of France.

Brodie watched Davidson; the possibility was tempting. But he was not easily persuaded.

"Ye have done business with Campbell in the past," Davidson pointed out.

"Aye, and his costs have taken most of the profit."

"I would need a guarantee," Davidson added. "In good faith, for a new business arrangement and the risk. Campbell will no' be pleased."

"That is my concern. Wot would ye require for the risk."

"Fifty cases of that particularly good whisky, with the profit to meself as a measure of good faith. The rest of wot ye could bring would go to market."

"Where are ye bound when ye leave?" Munro asked. "I would need to know which markets those might be before I entrust ye with any merchandise which is a far sight better than anything else ye might have."

"If I were to tell you that, you might attempt to make another arrangement yerself," Davidson replied.

Munro nodded. "Perhaps. But as my friend here said, I have no interest in doing so. There are other responsibilities that take my time. But I'll not do wrong by the person I work for, ye need to know that. And I'll go two dozen cases for yerself, the rest to market."

There was a long silence. Brodie he was beginning to think that Davidson wouldn't work with them.

"I'll be in Portsmouth for several days, waitin' on 'other cargo.' I leave the end of the second week. There's a man in Lisbon who will give a good price for the whisky. And I could be persuaded to pick up wine on my return, savin' ye that cost to another."

There was another long silence.

"You'll have the whisky by the time ye leave," Munro told him. "We'll negotiate for the wine then."

"Aye," Davidson agreed. "We have an agreement, and I'll count on ye bein' a Scot to honor it."

"And ye as well," Munro told him. "Now, wot of Duvalier?"

"Dinna know him by name, but there's a man seen around who does business of that sort—the sort the Royal Navy might like to know about."

"Smuggled cargo?" Brodie asked.

"Perhaps. I try to stay clear." He emphasized that he 'tried' to avoid it.

He seemed to sense the doubt.

"To my way of thinkin' it's poor business to risk losin' yer cargo and perhaps yer head, when there is plenty of business to go around. Aye?"

Munro nodded.

"But for some it seems the cargos the man deals in are worth the risk. This time it seemed the risk might be more."

"How is that?" Brodie asked.

"One of my men was about when the man you call Duvalier met the ship under cover of darkness; usually not necessary, and there's the risk of missing the landing on the changing tide and ending with a broken ship and a cargo in water."

"And ye just happened to be here as well," Munro commented.

Davidson smiled. "My crew was seeing to cargo we finished unloading earlier in the day. To make certain it was secure." Another smile. "From thieves."

"What makes ye think there was more risk with this particular cargo?"

"There was an accident on the dock." Davidson gestured to one of his men.

"Wot sort of accident?" Brodie asked.

"The workers he'd hired were hoisting a large crate from the hold of the ship," his man explained.

"This end of the port, there are no steam hoists," Davidson explained.

"The crate was large," the man continued. "It wasn't properly secured and it came down fast and hard on the dock, and broke apart." He shook his head.

"I never seen nothin' like that—there was a carved casket and one of them bodies all wrapped up."

"And weapons, most were iron, old, some pieces in copper, a curved sword, spears and such, along with broken pottery," Davidson explained.

"There was a stramash, as ye can well imagine. The one you call Duvalier was screamin' and cursin' that it cost him thousands of francs, and if he didna need them to finish the job he would have sent on them their way." He shrugged again.

"It's hard enough to find workers this side of the port that will work for less pay and the risk of the harbor patrols boardin' a ship. My crew also work the cargo for part of the profits.

"Not Duvalier," he continued. "It's the reason he gets the worst of the worst of the workers when he brings in cargo that the authorities might confiscate."

So, by the description Davidson's man had given, it seemed that Duvalier had recently received a shipment of smuggled artifacts. And taken them ... where?

Had they become part of the exhibit Sir Nelson was about to open at the museum?

According to Mikaela, the directors at the museum had been provided bills of lading, signed off by the Antiquities Department in Cairo, that verified the artifacts he had brought back with him. She had returned to verify the artifacts when she was attacked.

Who was there? And wot reason for the attack?

He knew more than when they left London. Duvalier had received a shipment of artifacts that he obviously didn't want the authorities to know about. It was safe to assume those artifacts were smuggled.

But for whom?

"If ye are satisfied, it would seem that our business is concluded," Davidson announced, and swiped the gold sovereigns into his other hand.

"Aye," Brodie replied.

"I will be expectin' those cases of whisky."

"Ye will have them before ye sail," Munro replied.

"Do ye believe him?" he asked as they left the tavern.

Brodie nodded as he glanced into the shadows at the entrance to a nearby inn.

"There is no reason for him to lie," he replied. "If he did, ye might be inclined to cancel yer business arrangement with him. Ye are takin' a risk with him."

"Lady Montgomery willna object," Munro replied. "And better Davidson than Campbell. It's worth the risk if there is a new market to be had on the Continent. And I intend to go with the cargo to make certain that it arrives safely."

Brodie had kept an eye on the street since they'd arrived, mindful of those they passed, particularly in a place like Portsmouth, a seaport, where those who made their way thieving were looking for the next victim. The back of his neck tingled the way it did when he was with the MET and on the chase of a criminal.

"Wot is it?" Munro said in a low voice.

Brodie's hand instinctively closed around the handle of the revolver as a man came out of the shadows behind them.

He shouted a warning to Munro and pushed him out of the way. Then another man, shorter than the first one, struck with a knife.

There was a warning shout as the shorter man seemed to have second thoughts when light from the street lamp gleamed off the barrel of the revolver Brodie had pulled from the front of his coat. And it was all over in a matter of seconds.

"Campbell or one of Davidson's men?" Brodie asked as he turned, and exclaimed, "Bloody hell!"

Munro was bent over, one hand pressed low at the front of his jacket. Blood gleamed dark in the light from the gas lamp.

"My guess would be Campbell." Munro's teeth gritted in pain. "Put off by inquirin' about Davidson. I never liked the man."

"Can ye walk?" Brodie asked.

"Aye," Munro replied, a tight sound between clenched teeth.

"We need to get out of here." He slipped an arm under Munro's shoulders. "Are ye sure ye can ye make it?"

Munro cursed in reply. "I can make it, if ye quit nattering and get on with it!"

Fourteen

THE STRAND

MIKAELA

I WORKED LATE, updating the chalkboard with the new information I had, with the intention of attempting to find Sophie Marquette the next day.

I had not heard from Brodie, but in truth I had been away from the office and a telephone most of the day.

He had said that he and Munro might be gone a couple of days, attempting to track down information at Portsmouth, where Mr. Brown had indicated they might be able to locate information regarding stolen artifacts that were coming into the country.

Mr. Cavendish brought supper from the public house, for which Rupert and I were exceedingly grateful.

"You are a bit like the hound that way," he declared. "No offense meant, miss, but he does have an appetite for Effie's meat pies."

Afterward, I decided to remain at the office for the night, as I had many times in the past. It was far more convenient when working on an inquiry case, and in the off chance that Brodie might call. He did not.

As the evening continued, I sat at the desk with my new typewriting machine, a smaller, much improved version that Brodie had purchased for me and had delivered to the office.

"For writing up yer notes and reports we need to provide from time to time," he explained in that off-hand manner that I had come to recognize was something very near shyness over something he had done for me. It was the same with the very expensive writing pen he had purchased for me, for 'scratching away at my notes.'

"So that yer not given to cursing when ye dinna have one with ye. I have had to explain that to more than one person."

That particular situation had only happened once, and, admittedly, I had said a rather colorful word at the time, more at myself for leaving from the office in a hurry to be off. And now a new typewriter.

Most women, my sister included, went all misty-eyed over flowers or some confection—deep, dark chocolate in Linnie's case.

I would take a typewriter and new pen over such things that either wilted or were consumed in a matter of days.

I pecked away for some time, then answered the door when there was a familiar scratching sound at the threshold, followed by Rupert's distinctive baying. I opened the door and he bounded past me and immediately deposited himself in front of the coal stove.

It had become a routine for him to accompany me whenever I was out and about across the city, particularly at night. He was my personal protection service that Brodie insisted upon. That and the revolver Brodie had given me.

"God help the poor soul who comes upon ye," he said at the time.

That was how I spent the evening, after placing a telephone call to my housekeeper at the townhouse in Mayfair to let her know that I would not be returning that night.

Mrs. Ryan had grown use to my stay-overs at the office after that first case when my sister and her daughter disappeared. It was such a deadly affair.

It was eventually solved and my sister found safe, but the tragedy of losing her own daughter made Mrs. Ryan particularly protective of me, to the extent that she even tolerated the hound on occasion.

It was very near midnight when I finished typing up my notes. I placed more coal on the stove, much to Rupert's approval, as he briefly raised his head, groaned, and went back to sleep.

It was better than having him on the bed in the adjacent room which Brodie forbade. There was something in that particular conversation about the advantage of sharing his bed with *me* rather than Rupert—something about warm feet on a cold night.

I checked the lock on the door and turned off the electric, then went into the room that had become our bedroom. I removed my boots, skirt, and shirtwaist, crawled under the covers, and went to sleep listening to Rupert snoring.

I have no way of knowing what time it was as I came up out of sleep in that way that something startles one awake, and discovered that the *something* was the sound of Rupert, on full alert, a far different sound when he was preparing to attack.

When Brodie was away, I kept the revolver on the floor just under the edge of the bed.

It sounded as if Rupert might tear the door down as I

threw back the covers, grabbed the revolver, and went into the outer office.

The hound persisted as glass in the door shattered and a hand reached through the opening and released the bolt. I raised the revolver and pulled back the hammer as the door slammed open and light from the gas lamp at the landing spilled through the doorway.

"For the love of God, Mikaela! Dinna shoot!"

I don't know who was more startled, me or the hound, as he finally sat down.

"You might have telephoned ..." I said as I turned on the electric at the desk and laid the revolver down. I turned around and saw Munro.

He was leaning over, supported by Brodie.

"Beg pardon, miss," he apologized, and would have fallen if Brodie hadn't held onto him.

"The other room ..." Brodie said as he angled his shoulder under Munro's and told him, "Just a bit further.

It took only a little more effort as he lowered Munro through the doorway and onto the bed and carefully eased him down. It was then I saw the bloodied bandage through the opening of Munro's jacket.

I have learned working inquiry cases with Brodie to expect almost anything. I have seen dead bodies, a good share of injuries and blood. I have even been shot at.

As he once explained it, most of it was boring, some of it interesting, and at times dangerous.

It was very near ten o'clock in the morning by the time Mr. Brimley finished attending Munro.

Brodie had sent Mr. Cavendish for him as soon as they had reached the Strand, after returning to London on the overnight train from Portsmouth, a decision Brodie made rather than remain there after the attack on the street.

It was in the aftermath of their return with Mr. Brimley's assurances that Munro would most definitely live that I had finally looked at Brodie where he stood at the foot of the bed, and discovered that he was covered in blood as well.

I have always had the ability to remain calm in the middle of a crisis, learned when I was quite young at my father's death, a gruesome discovery that no child should experience.

I had mastered the ability to close off shock or even horror at something, and never cried. That was something our father had insisted upon, even at the death of our mother.

And there was Brodie, who somehow had the ability to break down all my defenses.

"You're injured!" I exclaimed at the sight of yet more blood. I wasn't certain if I was terrified or furious.

"I'm all right," he insisted. "It's not me. The man bled all over the both of us."

After Mr. Brimley left with assurances that Munro would recover, Brodie had gone to the bath chamber across the landing and washed off the blood.

Afterward, Mr. Cavendish had brought breakfast from the public house.

I had dressed and sat across from Brodie as he downed a third cup of coffee, that dark gaze watching me as I waited for him to tell me what had happened.

"Ye could have been injured or worse answering the door in yer knickers," he commented.

I pointed out that I had the revolver, and not much risk of being attacked had it been someone else at the door.

"You could have been shot breaking in," I pointed out. "I doubt you would have made it past Rupert."

He nodded, exhaustion in the lines at the corners of eyes.

"True enough, but I couldna manage the key and my friend at the same time without causing him more injury," he admitted. "I'll wager Munro appreciated the view, though he would never admit it."

"I doubt that seeing a woman in her knickers is anything new for him," I replied.

All things considered, Munro seeing me in my petticoat and camisole was hardly a concern. I wanted to know what had happened in Portsmouth.

"Duvalier is most definitely involved in smuggling artifacts into the country," Brodie added as he finished explaining what they had learned in Portsmouth, that included their meeting with Campbell, and their meeting with a man by the name of Davidson.

"Do you trust this man, Davidson?"

"It's in his interest to tell the truth." He had also explained the new 'business arrangement' Munro had made with the man.

"Aye, I trust the information," he added.

"The question is, who is Duvalier smuggling the artifacts for?" I asked.

I thought of Sir Nelson, yet that made no sense. Unless he had hoped to add pieces to the exhibit he was not able to acquire otherwise.

However, a man like Duvalier, a known smuggler, would expect to be paid for any artifacts he had smuggled into the country which Sir Nelson did not have, according to everything we had learned so far.

The long and the short of it, as Brodie had often pointed out when looking at possible motive, was that smuggling was a dangerous business, for both the smuggler and the person receiving the smuggled items.

Items might be sold out from under a prospective purchaser—contrary to the old saying that there was 'honor among thieves.'

I suspected that honor had a price, if someone came along who offered more for something ... much like an auction. And there was always the risk that a shipment might be confiscated by the authorities. It did seem that had not happened. At the very least, not when the shipment arrived.

The shipment was obviously going somewhere after it left Portsmouth. The question was ... where?

"I thought of that," Brodie replied. "Alex Sinclair may be able to assist with that. The Agency has access to information that could be useful."

The Agency, specifically the Special Services Agency that we both had contact with in past inquiry cases, and not always with the most favorable results. Specifically, he had very nearly been killed during a previous inquiry case.

It was the difference between how a man or woman looked at things.

Brodie could be quite circumspect about such things. Case in point, he had survived the situation. In the aftermath, he was more careful when the agency was involved, mindful that Sir Avery often had other motives in the assistance he provided from time to time.

For myself, I had no tolerance for others' secrets or hidden motives. As far as I was concerned, once trust was broken, it was broken, and I was done with that person.

Of course, that did present an issue when other assistance was necessary. And I did like Alex, who worked at said agency, very much. He was quite endearing with his spectacles and unruly hair, his gadgets and inventions, most particularly a coding machine that I found to be quite fascinating.

"Very well," I stiffly replied to Brodie's suggestion, knowing full well that he would do as he pleased. Stubborn man!

I stood before the board to make certain that I had added everything we'd learned.

"There might be something Sophie Marquette could tell us," I suggested.

I had explained what I learned from Templeton, and suggested there might be something to learn about Duvalier from the woman.

When there was no response to my suggestion, I turned from the board.

Brodie sat at his desk, arms crossed over his chest, head slumped forward ... asleep.

So much for any objections to my calling on Sophie Marquette.

According to Templeton's information, Sophie stayed in one of the rooms let by the theater during a production.

I was familiar with the location from a past case. It was in the theater district, not far from the Strand.

I had thought of taking the hound with me, more to ease Brodie's concerns than anything else. However, he was not about. Undoubtedly off scavenging the local business establishments. It was a favorite pastime.

Mr. Cavendish waved down a driver and I climbed aboard. He gave me the familiar 'fish-eye,' as I called it, along with a frown.

"You might wait until Mr. Brodie can accompany you," he suggested.

Dear man. He was much like a protective uncle, or at least what I thought one might be like, as I never had a protective uncle, or a protective father, for that matter.

"He knows of it," I assured him. "It's very near in the theater district. I won't be long."

That look again as I gave the driver the location at Covent Garden.

The tenant buildings on the street adjacent to the garden had once been made of red brick; however, *red* was a misnomer, as they were covered with the usual soot from coal fires and grime of the city, and now a dingy brown.

From the information Templeton provided, Sophie Marquette had appeared in a brief production at the Adelphi, and in a minor role at Drury Lane. She lived in the building at Number Twelve Broad Court, which was on the crescent very near the Garden as she apparently waited for her next role.

Which raised the obvious question, how much, if anything, did she know about Duvalier's smuggling activities? I might very well be on a fool's errand.

The driver found the building at the address and I paid him, climbed the steps to the entrance, and stepped inside the foyer

I had no room number; however, I had found in the past that there was usually a housekeeper or other person in one of the ground floor flats who collected the rents for the landlord.

"Who might you be lookin' for?" A woman with a wash bucket and mop had appeared at a back entrance.

I explained that I was an acquaintance of Sophie Marquette and had stopped by to call on her.

"Calls herself an actress," the woman snorted. "Seems to me she spends more time with the men. I suppose that's entertainin'."

"I'd like to leave a message under the door, if you could give me her room number."

"I s'pose there's no harm. Room number four, up the way on the second floor," she replied. Then she added, "it's been a busy mornin' for her; good that she'll be on her way. I run a respectable place here, and don't like trouble. I wouldn't be able to rent no rooms with the likes of her carrying on."

Sophie Marquette had given notice that she would be leaving?

There was a bit more conversation as I made my way up to the second floor, the sort of conversation that included the woman's miseries, issues with other tenants, and another comment about 'theater people,' as the door to a ground floor apartment snapped shut behind the woman.

I found the room number and would have knocked at the door. However, it was already open. Was it possible that Sophie was about to leave?

I called out, when it seemed she had not heard me.

Brodie has said in the past that I have a natural talent for crime, and not in a complimentary way. Usually a pithy comment and the certainty that I might be hiding a criminal past. I did have a penchant for finding myself in the middle of a situation. I preferred to call it curiosity.

Curiosity threw me back against the wall in the hallway as the door suddenly flew open and a man rushed past.

Another word Brodie used came to mind—*reckless*, and usually accompanied by a curse as I reacted instinctively and thrust out a foot. It caught the man on his boot and he stumbled. He rolled, found his footing again, lunged for the stairwell, and scrambled down.

I went after him in spite of Brodie's warnings in the past.

He had already reached the street, as the woman I had seen earlier opened the door to her flat.

When I reached the street, the man was gone, no doubt using the traffic of trams and cabs to disappear.

Who was he? Another 'friend' of Sophie's, as the matron had indicated? Duvalier perhaps?

I returned to the building and the second floor, hoping that Sophie might be persuaded to tell me who the man was.

Or not, as I entered the room and discovered Sophie Marquette's body in the middle of the floor in a pool of blood that slowly spread across the floor.

Anything I hoped that I might learn was gone.

Brodie has said in the past that I have a peculiar nature when it came to dead things—not at all bothered by bodies or the sight of blood. I knew, of course, where it came from.

Things experienced as a young child did have a tendency to stay with one. And while the sight of a body could be startling when one came upon it unexpectedly, for me there was simply an acceptance, and an odd curiosity, as he called it. Almost as if I was detached from it.

That curiosity was there now as I spied the piece of paper that appeared just at the edge of Sophie Marquette's gloved hand.

"Step away, miss!" The voice of authority called from the hallway.

I quickly tucked the paper inside the sleeve of my jacket, then slowly stood.

"Turn around, slowly, and show me yer hands."

"That's her," the housekeeper peered around the constable's shoulder. "That's the one I saw."

"Don't be ridiculous," I replied. "There was a man here when I arrived."

"I didn't see no one else. That's her, officer. That's the one came askin' for the poor girl."

Now it was 'poor girl.'

"I can explain ..." I would have said, but the constable cut me off.

"You can explain to the magistrate."

I made another attempt, only to find my wrists bound in manacles.

"As I said, miss. You can explain to the magistrate. And wot is this? A revolver?"

Fifteen

I HAVE EXPERIENCED a great many things in my somewhat unconventional upbringing, after my great aunt brought my sister and me to live with her as children.

There are my travels, of course, that took me to many fascinating and occasionally dangerous places. There is the success of my Emma Fortescue novels.

Then there are the inquiry cases with Brodie, not the usual sort of partnership between two people, for certain. That was certainly another adventure which I had assumed would never happen in my life, as the gossip of those in polite society and the tomes of the British press had pointed out—who would possibly tolerate an often-scandalous carrying-on by a woman?

Scandalous indeed. And now arrested by the Metropolitan Police, an entirely new experience.

I sat in the room at the Bow Street Police Station with a guard at the door should I attempt to flee, desperate criminal that I was, 'detained' in the matter of Sophie Marquette's murder.

Detained was such an interesting word. Not arrested precisely, nor formally charged. Yet.

It was very much like a disobedient child being denied supper and sent off to my room. Except this room was stark and dingy. There were bars on the window along with the guard at the door, and the impending arrival of someone I was not at all certain I wanted to see.

I had requested the sergeant contact the person who seemed most appropriate under the circumstances upon my arrival, so that he could explain that I was most likely not the murderer. That person was Inspector Dooley.

He had worked with Brodie in the past and was more than aware of our private inquiries on behalf of clients.

Inspector Dooley had arrived in good time and had me transferred from the holding cell I had been taken to when I arrived—another unique experience—to my present accommodation until he could contact Brodie.

I was not in complete agreement on that, considering I was fairly certain what Brodie's reaction would be. In spite of the fact that I had demonstrated more than once that I was quite well prepared to defend myself.

I heard voices now from the hallway beyond that door that had been secured against any attempt to escape. A voice with that very familiar Scots accent.

The door was unlocked and opened by my guard, and the man belonging to that accent appeared at the doorway.

He had that expression I was familiar with, his police inspector expression, which is to say no expression at all, except for a slight frown as the constable handed him a piece of paper. My official release from police custody, I imagined.

The constable nodded then turned and disappeared down the hallway.

"Come along," Brodie said with that same demeanor.

I might have been mistaken. but I thought I caught a hint of a smile.

I gathered my bag, which the constable who arrested me had gone through quite thoroughly and quickly discovered the revolver.

I had pointed out quite reasonably on the ride to the Bow Street station in a police van that I could hardly be the murderer as Sophie Marquette's throat had been cut, and the only pieces of cutlery in the room were forks and spoons scattered about. The young woman had obviously not been killed with a spoon, and I was not covered in blood. For all the good it did me.

Brodie escorted me down the hallway to a desk where paperwork waited. It seemed it was quite a process to obtain my release.

"Remanded into your custody, Mr. Brodie," the sergeant announced. "No bail required."

Remanded into his custody?

I was certain I caught that trace of humor at the slight twitch at one corner of Brodie's mouth. He signed the paperwork and was handed my revolver.

"It can be dangerous to carry a weapon about, particularly with a woman," the sergeant commented. "You might want to keep it locked away, if you get my meanin', sir."

His meaning was quite clear as he glanced over at me.

"Aye," Brodie replied.

We reached the street and he waved down a driver. When the cabman arrived, he opened the gate. I stepped past him and up into the cab. He took the seat beside me, and gave the driver the address of the office on the Strand.

"It is fortunate the sergeant was able to reach Mr. Dooley," he commented. "Otherwise, the situation could have been far different and not to yer liking. The police encounter all sorts of disreputable women on the streets."

I did my best to ignore that. He was enjoying this far too much.

"I did consider telling him to keep ye for a while."

"I can explain," I replied.

There was definitely amusement in that dark gaze.

"Munro was in no condition to be left alone," I pointed out. "You had nodded off, and there was our inquiry case to attend to. I thought Sophie Marquette might be able to tell me something that could be important."

"So," he replied in that way that always meant there was more. "I'm responsible that you were discovered where a woman had been murdered and taken into custody by the police."

Not precisely what I meant, yet I was more than willing to go along with that.

"You have frequently told me that time is of the essence in solving a crime," I reminded him. "And Sophie Marquette was a known companion of Duvalier. It did seem important to speak with her to find out what she might know."

"And wot was she able to tell ye after ye found her dead?"

More sarcasm. It did seem to be a particular characteristic of Scots. Yet, two could play this game. I retrieved the note I had found tucked inside Sophie Marquette's glove and handed it to him.

"Wot is this?"

"It is what Sophie Marquette was able to 'tell me,' even though she was already dead," I replied with equal sarcasm.

"It's in French."

"So it is. Would you like me to translate it?"

He shook his head. "I dinna know the reason I put up with ye."

I smiled. "Of course you do."

"Och, ye are a brazen hussy. I ought to bend ye over me knee."

"You must admit, I am quite good at finding clues."

"That has yet to be seen. Wot does the message say?" He handed it back to me.

I smiled to myself.

"It would appear that it could be from Duvalier. It's about meeting someone and what appears to be a location." I frowned.

"What location?"

"Dover." I looked up.

"It would seem that the woman was to meet Duvalier in Dover, and leave from there."

"Two days. The housekeeper said that she had given notice that she was leaving today, and she had packed a bag."

"Aye, two days. Apparently Duvalier planned for the shipment to be delivered, then collect his fee for it."

The question was, where was it to be delivered and what was in the shipment?

Mr. Cavendish greeted us as we arrived at the office.

"Good to see that you're all right, miss."

It did seem that he was well informed regarding my 'incarceration.'

I thanked him and knelt to scratch the hound behind the ears as he came to greet me as well.

"Mr. Brimley was here after you left, to see to Mr. Munro," he went on to tell Brodie.

"And there was a young man a short while ago. He said it was about information you were asking about. He left a message with Mr. Munro."

I exchanged a look with Brodie.

Was it possible Alex had been able to learn something about that shipment from Portsmouth? I quickly followed Brodie up the stairs to the office.

Munro sat at the desk. He wore a shirt of Brodie's, loosely buttoned over the bandages that Mr. Brimley had applied. He looked none the worse for wear in spite of the injury he'd received.

There was a fire in the coal stove and a carton of food before him, no doubt from the Public House. He grimaced slightly as he made an attempt to stand. I laid a hand on his shoulder.

"There is no need to stand on my account," I assured him.

"Good to see you, miss. None the worse for yer experience, aye?" he asked.

"It was very ... enlightening," I replied.

"Ye should have gone out the window," he commented with an amused expression.

I had done exactly that with Brodie in Paris on a previous inquiry case. Not something I would recommend—loose drainpipes, the French police very near, and a body in the room we hastily departed.

"I'm afraid there wasn't time—however I did discover something that was important at the time."

"Dinna encourage her," Brodie commented. "It's bad enough she was taken into custody."

"Aye, a common criminal." The smile on Munro's face deepened.

"What of the information Alex Sinclair was able to find?" I asked.

"He was able to verify the shipment from Portsmouth two nights ago. The warehouseman recognized the driver and made note of the name of the company—Hodges Hauling Service, and it was signed for by the driver with initials S.T."

"The destination?" Brodie asked.

Munro shook his head.

"S.T.?" I commented.

I saw the look that passed between Brodie and Munro.

"Whoever is behind this is moving quickly," Brodie said.

"Aye, loose ends," Munro commented.

"What are loose ends?" I asked.

"It would seem that whoever is behind the smuggled ship-ment is getting rid of those involved in order to protect himself," Munro explained. "Loose ends. It would explain the woman's murder."

It was a chilling thought.

"How are we to find who is behind all of this?"

"To know the mind of a thief, ye have to think like one," Munro explained. "And go where they go."

"Where would a thief take a shipment of smuggled arti-facts?" I asked. "It isn't as if they can be carried about in a hat box."

"There is one way to find out," Brodie replied.

I followed him into the adjacent bedroom, where he changed into other clothes—those he wore when going 'out and about' on the street, as he called it.

The transformation was quite remarkable. It was always a surprise, how easily he moved back into that world. Except for that dark gaze under the brim of the cap he pulled on, I might not have recognized him.

"Let me help," I told him.

He looked up after pulling on worn, scuffed boots that he refused to part with in spite of the fact they were worn through at the soles. He had refused to let me send them out to the bootmaker for repair.

"This is not fer you, and there will be no argument about it. Ye need to stay with Munro." He touched my cheek. "Are ye worrit about that curse?"

And when I didn't reply, there was that half smile. I reached into the pocket of my skirt and retrieved the amulet Mr. Hosni had given me.

"Please take this." I handed to him.

"I dinna believe in curses, lass."

Nevertheless, he took it.

I followed him back into the office where he checked his revolver and tucked it into the waist of his trousers.

Munro would have stood to go with him. Brodie shook his head.

"I'll not have ye bleedin' all over the place again," he told him. "I need ye to stay here."

Something more passed between them in Gaelic, and ended with a colorful remark from Munro. I had my suspicions of course. Possibly something about keeping an eye on me.

Brodie kissed me, a light brush of his mouth on mine.

"How long will you be?" I asked, a ridiculous question of course. There was no way of knowing. His reply?

"Take care of my friend. Send for Mr. Brimley if the bleeding starts again."

I stared at the door after he had gone.

Afterward I went to the chalkboard and added the information we now had. Not that it was necessary, I had made notes in my notebook.

I straightened the desk, put more coal on the coal stove, and brewed another pot of coffee—the extent of my cooking skills.

"Ye are fidgetin'," Munro commented as I set a cup before him. "Ye know as well as I do it will be a while before he returns."

"Yes, of course."

He was right. I knew from the cases I had been part of that it might take hours for him to locate the transport company and make his inquiries. And then ...?

"Are you comfortable?" I asked.

"Well enough, miss," he assured me, as he sat back in Brodie's chair.

I went to my own desk, where I might work on my next novel or type up a report on the typewriter Brodie had purchased for me.

The problem was that I had finished my last Emma Fortescue novel the week before and sent it off to James Warren, my publisher. It was a thinly disguised account of our last inquiry case. I hadn't yet started the next episode of that very accomplished young woman's adventures.

I 'pecked away' at the keys, as Brodie called it.

Emma Fortescue was not easily frightened; however, this night was different. It was the first time he had gone out alone hunting for the smugglers who had stolen the chest that contained that ancient secret.

I glanced at the clock at the wall beside Brodie's desk. It was half-past eight of the evening ...

Three people had been murdered, with a fourth person badly injured and near death ...

My publisher was convinced that my readers were fasci-nated by the murder mysteries Emma Fortescue had embarked upon. The sales had been quite remarkable.

There were few clues except for those who had been murdered, two men in a most ghastly fashion, and the woman with a cryptic note found tucked in the sleeve of her jacket ...

Who could have killed them? What was in that stolen chest that was worth three lives? And now?

The bell at the landing rang furiously.

Brodie had it installed for Mr. Cavendish to announce that someone had arrived.

"Wot the devil is the man up to now?" Munro said as he came out of the chair at Brodie's desk.

When I started toward the door, he stopped me, and shook his head as the bell continued to ring.

He retrieved the knife he always carried, then went to the door, the bell still ringing. He yanked the door.

"You can tell the fellow below to quit ringin' the bloody bell—it's enough to wake the dead! As for the damned dog ... he tried to take me leg off!"

"Wot the devil are ye doin' here?" Munro demanded of the man who filled the door opening.

"I heard you were dead."

Mr. Brown replied as casual as if he were discussing the weather, as he pushed his way into the office.

"Ye heard wrong," Munro replied.

"Where's Brodie?" Brown demanded.

"He's not here."

Brown cursed.

"Wot is it?" Munro demanded. "Wot's happened?'

Sixteen

BRODIE

HE FOUND Hodges Transport easily enough, not far from Waterloo Station.

It was a small operation compared to more well-known companies with wagons and vans that crisscrossed London daily.

A faded sign hung over the entrance to what passed for an office. There was a side yard across an alley, with two wagons and the horses that pulled them.

A lanky lad closed the gate behind him and crossed the alley to that small office.

A woman behind the counter looked up as he entered the office that was in fact no more than a counter with a coal stove in one corner and a doorway at the back, no doubt to a storeroom or possibly a room where the owner lived.

"We made the last run of the day if yer here about a shipment," the woman told him, with a weariness that was familiar in the streets of the East End.

"I can set somethin' up for first thing in the mornin', if it suits you." There was a long look.

"If it's work yer after," she continued, "I could use a man, with me husband laid up with the rheumatism and only Gilley here to pick up the extra work."

Brodie shook his head. "I'm here about a shipment picked up last night from the rail station. Yer company name was shown on the papers, signed for by someone with the letters S.T."

"S.T.?" the lad replied.

He was tall but thin, no more than fourteen or fifteen years by the scattering of chin hairs. Already a man with a man's responsibilities, Brodie thought.

"That be Sam Turner," Gilley added.

The woman made a disgusted sound. "And now no doubt layin' somewhere drunk, the reason I'm short a driver. What's yer interest in the shipment?" she asked.

"It's gone missin'." Closer to the truth than not. "And the man I work for sent me. If ye can help with information where it was delivered ..." Brodie took out a coin and placed it on the counter.

The woman looked at him with suspicion, snatched up the coin and dropped it into a drawer behind the counter.

"It wasn't on the log," she explained. "I didn't know about it until this mornin'. Gilley here sleeps in the harness shed. He heard Sam take off with a wagon after his last run last night and not a word about it.

"He found the wagon and the team in the yard this mornin', but no sign of Sam, and good riddance, I say. I need a driver I can rely on."

She eyed him sharply. "Are ye sure you don't need some extra work? Or might know someone who does?"

Brodie shook his head. "Do ye know where Sam might be? Where he lives?"

She shook her head. "He mentioned a woman he kept company with once, but never said where. Lately he took to the shed with Gilley. I got the feelin' there weren't no woman. Not that it's any surprise. He gets his pay and he's into the drink.

"Not something a woman would put up with, if you know what I mean," she added, "You certain you couldn't use some work? You look fit enough."

"What about you?" he asked Gilley. "Some place he might have mentioned where he might go of an evenin'?"

He saw way the lad's expression changed, the glance that slid to the woman. Gilley shook his head.

There was something there, but it was obvious the lad wouldn't say.

"I thank ye," he told the woman.

He gave Gilley a long look, tipped his cap, and left the freight office.

The lad caught up with him on the street.

"I didn't want to say nothin' in front of Mrs. Hodge," Gilley explained. "She goes hard on Sam and he needs the work when he's not in the drink."

"Do ye know where I might find him?"

Gilley nodded. "You might try the Hole in the Wall tavern. It's just over the way under the tracks where the trains make the turn-about. I've brought him back from there often enough."

He thanked Gilley and handed him a coin. He refused at first.

"I like Sam. He's been good to me, showin' me the way with the horse team and how to make me way around the other haulers that would like to put Mrs. Hodge out of business."

"Ye take it," Brodie insisted.

"I thank you kindly," Gilley told him. "With what I make haulin' freight … well, I appreciate it. Not that you would understand."

"More than ye know," Brodie told him.

Gilley tipped his cap and turned back to that small building tucked back from the street.

Brodie followed the lad's instructions and found the tavern with the rumble of railcars passing overhead.

The Hole in the Wall was just that, a hole in a stone wall with a sign over and light in the windows, and the familiar sounds and smells of a tavern.

Inside, workers gathered at the tables, and two- and three-deep at the bar, as pints of ale were set down by the barman.

He made his way to the end of the bar and ordered a pint of ale.

"Sam Turner? A friend told me he could be found here."

The barman gestured across the tavern to a table at a niche in the wall, as another train rumbled overhead and shook the wood floor underfoot.

"He's been here since late last night, had a special job, he said. Still there this mornin'. Now he's still here, not that I object when a man wants to spend his money."

Brodie nodded and retrieved the mug of ale set before him. He made his way through the chaos of conversation, hoots of laughter, and more than a few curses, to that niche in the wall.

He pulled out a chair and sat at the table. "Sam Turner?"

The man stared at him. "Do I know you?"

Brodie set the mug on the table. Ale was not his first choice, and not on this night when he needed to keep his wits about him.

He eyed the man across from him. There were dozens of

men just like him across the city, who worked in the factories, docks, and back of shops. And more often for just enough coin to purchase that next pint when they should have gone home to a family and paid the rent or the grocer for enough food to get through another day.

"Ye picked up a shipment late last night from the rail station."

"Who told ye that?" Turner managed to reply.

"Gilley told me. He's worrit about ye, said ye didn't come in today." Close enough to the truth, the lad was worried for the man.

"Ah, Gilley. He's a good lad," Turner replied as he waved a hand overhead, a signal for another pint.

A young girl appeared eventually, squeezing her way through the crowd of customers as another train rattled the mug she set on the table. Brodie paid for it. She smiled and disappeared back toward the bar.

"I can pay for me own drink," Sam Turner said.

"That last run of the night from the station must have paid well."

"Well enough," Turner agreed.

"From Portsmouth, ye say."

Not that Turner had said. But he wouldn't know that in his condition.

The man took a drink and nodded. "I kept the wagon out late so Ms. Hodge wouldn't know. She would have wanted the whole fee," he explained with a wink at Brodie.

"Not that she deserved any of it, but I've a bit left over for Gilley. He's a good lad."

Brodie continued to play the part. "I'd sure like to find a job like that, even if it was for one night."

Turner nodded over his mug. "The man never gave his name, jus' said that he needed a driver."

"Wot did he look like? A tall sort, an accent?" Brodie suggested. An associate of Duvalier's perhaps?

Turner nodded. "An accent sure enough, one of them foreign sorts." He laid a finger aside his nose.

"But I know how to handle 'em. He was a short, wiry fellow, stopped me at the gate when I came in after the last delivery of the evenin'. Said there was a good fee in it just to pick up a shipment that come in from Portsmouth at the rail station." He patted the pocket of his worn jacket.

"Sure enough, ten pounds. I'd be lucky to see that much in a year." Turner took another long drink of ale and smiled, no doubt at the thought of his newfound wealth that was rapidly disappearing in mugs of ale.

"Where were ye to deliver the shipment? Some company, a warehouse perhaps, for a fee like that?"

Sam Turner looked over at him through blood-shot eyes and grinned.

"That was the beauty of it, my friend. I had to deliver it to the river. For ten pounds!" He chuckled and almost went over.

"A dangerous place for certain," Brodie replied as he righted the man once more in the chair.

"Fer some," Turner shrugged. He grew serious.

"I wasn't there long. There was a boat waiting at the landing just after the bridge."

Brodie nodded as he made a mental note of what Turner was telling him.

"Must have been good-sized for a large cargo."

Was it possible the man knew where it was bound? Something overheard?

Turner leaned closer with a gaping smile.

"True enough." He took another drink and smiled. "Curious I was, who would pay that much for a delivery. I watched from the high street after I left. Wot sort of cargo was worth what the man paid me to deliver it, I asked meself. And how was one man lame at one leg to go about it?" He poked Brodie in the arm.

"There was others there, waitin'. They loaded the cargo on a boat and crossed the water easy enough. But only as far as the island." He winked.

"I know because I saw the lantern when they made landing there."

"An island? In the middle of the river?" Brodie made a scoffing sound as he continued to listen.

"There are several islands up the north where some of the rich people have places. But not this island." Turner reached across the table for the mug of ale in front of Brodie.

"No sense lettin' it get warm," he said as he took a drink.

"Wot about the island?" Brodie asked, determined to get as much information as possible from him.

"It's covered with trees and grass, and rock, you see." The words slurred. "What ye can't see is what's left of an old stone tower, built a long time ago."

Turner smiled again and nodded, his eyes closing as he swayed in the chair.

Brodie steadied him once more. Turner patted him on the shoulder.

"Tell Gilley ... I'll be round in the mornin'," he said as he slumped forward on the table and began to snore.

A man with a limp who paid Sam Turner ten pounds to deliver that shipment from Portsmouth. An island in the middle of the river that could only be reached by boat, and an old stone tower. The perfect place to hide a shipment of smuggled artifacts.

He tucked a gold crown in Sam Turner's pocket, stopped the barmaid on his way out of the Hole in the Wall tavern, and gave her a half crown.

"See that he has food, and a place for the night."

She stared after him as he left.

The railroad tracks rumbled overhead with the next train that made the turn around over the Hole in the Wall tavern as Brodie made his way toward the river.

Seventeen

I DIDN'T like Mr. Brown. I certainly didn't trust him. His reputation precluded any of that. Still ...

He had provided valuable information in the past, and again regarding Duvalier and that smuggled shipment in Portsmouth.

"Where's Brodie?" he again demanded.

I caught the change of expression on Munro's face. Not that he trusted Brown either; however he had worked with him in the past. I had learned that in pieces of conversation, bits of information that were revealed. I knew not to ask questions, most particularly when it came to my great aunt's business dealings that Munro managed for her.

"We have the name of the transport company that picked up the shipment at Waterloo. Brodie went to see what information they have about that smuggled cargo."

Brown nodded. "I heard you'd returned from Portsmouth. One of my men picked up a rumor of goods being moved on the river tonight."

On the river? And moved some other place? Had Brodie been able to learn that as well?

"By whom?" I asked.

"None you would want to cross paths with, Lady Forsythe," Brown replied as he crossed to the desk. He grabbed the glass of whisky I'd poured earlier.

"Pirates, and a bloody dangerous lot they are," he said as he drained the glass.

"Pirates?"

I would have laughed except he was quite serious as he nodded in Munro's direction. He held up the empty tumbler.

"You have some experience with them and her ladyship's whisky."

Munro nodded. "Some."

"And ye know their ways." Brown turned to me and smiled, as very near as I supposed that was possible.

"It's always a matter of beating them at their own game."

"And that would be?"

That smile again.

"Beat them at their own game, for a price that is."

I looked over at Munro. I trusted him. As for Mr. Brown ...

Under the circumstances it did not seem that we had much choice. Brodie was out there, very possibly walking into a very dangerous situation.

"And the reason yer here now?" Munro asked.

That smile again that would have made anyone uneasy.

"Brodie has helped me in the past, as you well know, and in spite of the fact that he was with the MET. We might have been on opposite sides of certain things, but in spite of that, he is the only man I have ever respected or trusted. I don't want to see him cut down by a bunch of thieves and cutthroats, or that cargo fall into the wrong hands, you might say."

Honor among thieves? I thought.

He approached where I stood, and Munro moved closer as well.

To protect me?

Under the circumstances, with that wound he'd received, it wasn't something I wanted to risk.

As for Brown ... he was stout, with a fringe of brown hair around a balding head under the cap he wore, and a thick beard streaked with grey. His clothes were that of the street—black trousers and a gray cotton shirt over thick arms, very much the same as Brodie often wore when he wanted to go about unseen.

The resemblance ended there. There were deep lines on Brown's face with two rather nasty scars that, considering his reputation and 'line of work,' were not surprising. His brown eyes narrowed now as he watched me, much like a cat watching a mouse that it might pounce on at any moment.

He glanced down at the revolver in my hand and there was that smile again—almost, but not quite, and I thought of Lewis Carroll's Cheshire cat.

"I heard that you know how to use it." The smile deepened. He reached out and grabbed me by the chin.

"Pretty and dangerous. If Brodie hadn't married you, I might consider it myself."

My fingers tightened around the handle of the revolver.

"And not lived to tell of it."

He roared with laughter and took a step back as Munro moved between us.

"Wot else do ye know?" Munro demanded.

Brown continued to stare at me.

"The rumor is that a cargo will be moved tonight."

"Where?" Munro again demanded.

"The landing at Waterloo Bridge, and a strip of land—an abandoned island, just beyond. Only, not so abandoned—the perfect hiding place for smuggled cargo. And if Brodie is there ...?" he shook his head.

"Aye," Munro replied. "How many men are with ye?"

"Enough, with some already sent there," Brown replied.

Munro nodded as he retrieved that blood-stained jacket he'd worn the night before as he and Brodie left Portsmouth.

I went into the adjacent bedroom and quickly changed into a pair of trousers and a shirt that I'd worn before on a previous inquiry case. I had discovered very quickly the advantage, and put the revolver into one of the pockets.

"What is this?" Brown demanded as I returned and grabbed an old jacket from the coat stand.

Munro moved with some effort as he checked the knife he kept hidden in his boot, and then looked up.

"I'm going with you," I told him. I was prepared for an argument from him, I saw it in his expression. However, there was none.

"It's no place for a woman," Brown snapped.

"You're quite right, of course," I told him. I wasn't about to remain at the office, sitting on my hands, as it were, while Brodie was out there possibly walking alone into a very dangerous situation.

"You could be injured. I'll not answer to Brodie for it."

I didn't bother to respond to that as I quickly braided my hair and pulled on one of Brodie's caps that I found on top of the cabinet where he'd tossed it.

Brown swore. "I'll not risk my men over a foolish woman. I forbid it."

"Nevertheless."

Munro made a sound that sounded very much like Brodie as I pushed past Brown to the door.

"Do you trust his information?" I asked Munro as we entered the rented hack Mr. Cavendish had found for us. We were to meet Brown and his men a distance apart from that landing, just beyond Waterloo Bridge.

"I trust his greed. He'd not risk his own men on a fool's errand."

"What if Brodie's not there?"

That sharp blue gaze met mine in the light that spilled in from a streetlamp we passed.

"More's the reason that ye will leave."

We passed the rest of the ride in silence.

Waterloo Bridge was very near the Strand at the Victoria Embankment. It connected the city of London to the West End. Electric lights gleamed along the promenade at the gardens that fronted Whitehall.

There was only light traffic on the bridge, a horse-drawn tram returning to the city proper, and a handful who chose to cross afoot.

Below on that dark ribbon of water, a steamboat passed under one of the arches and continued downriver as we sped into the waiting darkness on the other side of the river.

When we reached the other side, the driver left the roadway at the Waterloo embankment, then swung the hack onto a dirt road, the horses' hooves muffled.

It was like entering a different world, with the towering stack of a smelting plant looming up out of the darkness beneath the sliver of the moon overhead, as we passed other low buildings, fishing shacks, and a warehouse.

The driver pulled to a stop, and I heard the faint whickering sound of other horses at a nearby wagon and hack, with the gleam of a weapon drawn as our driver pulled alongside.

Brown and his men had arrived ahead, and a large shadow that could only be the smuggler loomed up out the darkness.

"One of my men went ahead," Brown said in a low voice. "They're here with a boat anchored at the other side of the island."

By that, it could only mean the river pirates.

"There's a path across to the island at the bottom of the embankment," he said in a low voice. "With the tide out, we'll cross on foot."

I caught the faint movement of light out on the island. A lantern perhaps. Duvalier's men? Or the pirates after that smuggled cargo?

That sharp gaze fastened on me.

"What's she doin' here?" he snapped.

"None of yer concern!" Munro replied.

"Yer responsibility then," Brown muttered. "But she's to stay here. I won't have her causin' trouble out on the island."

Trouble? When I would have said something, Munro stopped me with a hand on my arm.

"What of Brodie?" he asked.

"If he's here, he's already out on the island." Brown turned to follow the rest of his men down the embankment.

"If need be, ye can tie her to the wagon."

He was gone, his shadow melting into the surrounding darkness.

I felt the urgency as Munro's hand tightened on my arm.

"I agreed for ye to come this far, but yer to stay here," he told me, barely a whisper. "I dinna know what we'll find on that island, and I'll not have my friend to answer to afterward for bringing ye."

Not an idle threat.

He was right of course, and I might have reminded him that he was in no condition to accompany Brown to whatever waited out on the island.

I didn't ... I knew better. He was very much like Brodie in that. Instead, I reluctantly agreed. And he too was gone, disappearing after Brown down the embankment.

I had every intention of keeping my word, if it hadn't been for the sudden flare of light on the island—a torch perhaps, immediately followed by an explosion that lit up the embankment, the water that surrounded the island, and that narrow causeway.

I thought of Brodie and then Munro, perhaps both of them out there, and I was already running down the embankment

I reached the water's edge and a small landing, the light from that explosion gleaming on the watery causeway Brown had spoken of. I could see those out on the island, a swarm of dark figures amid another explosion, and heard the distinctive sound of steel blade against steel blade, and gunfire.

I ran across that narrow slip of land, the mud sucking at my boots as I reached the island. I saw Munro. I pulled the revolver from the pocket of my trousers.

He cursed as I caught up with him. There was more, of course, undoubtedly something about my going back to the wagons. Instead, he shook his head, that sharp blue gaze scanning the battle at the foot of the tower.

"Yer to stay behind me." There was no time for more as the fighting surged toward us. His hand tightened as he pulled me with him, a knife in his other hand.

I had been caught up in dangerous encounters before, but nothing like the one that engulfed the island.

We reached the far edge of the battle toward the far side of the island and he thrust me into the shelter of trees and low-hanging branches. I tried to stop him.

"Stay here!"

The tower was engulfed in flames as he went back and quickly disappeared in that fighting swarm of bodies, along with more gunfire.

Through billowing clouds of smoke and flames, I saw the figure of a man escape and turn toward that opposite embankment of the river, followed by another, shorter one who limped and hopped like a small dark crow ...

The memory was there from days earlier—the worker I'd glimpsed at the museum just outside the Egyptian exhibit before it opened!

I glanced back toward the tower in the hope of finding Munro, but there was no sight of him.

Who was the man who now fled? Who had no doubt arranged for that shipment of smuggled artifacts? Was Duvalier with him? Or had he already received payment for his services?

Blood money, I thought. And the person responsible was about to escape.

I should stay where I was. It was dangerous to leave shelter with the fighting that surrounded the tower. Still ...

I thought of the brutal murders of Sir Nelson and Mr. Hosni, the sad loss of both who had dedicated their lives to providing a glimpse of the Egyptian culture to the world with no reward for themselves.

What of that stolen wood box and Sophie Marquette's death?

Nothing more than loose ends, Brodie had called it. And now two people were escaping. I ran from the cover of the trees toward the place where I had seen them.

The edge of another embankment sloped down to a landing as those two figures made their way down to the water and a boat that waited. It rode deep in the water as a steam engine sputtered to life.

It seemed that stolen shipment was already on board, and I followed down the embankment, then stopped at a warning shout.

It was not for me, but for the smaller man with that familiar limp, who suddenly turned back. Light from the fire at the tower gleamed off the blade of the knife in his hand.

A shot rang out as I raised the revolver, and the man with the knife stared with gaping mouth and fell to ground. I instinctively spun around, my hands tightening over the handle of the revolver.

"If ye fire the damned thing, ye make yerself a widow."

I knew that voice, that narrowed dark gaze as Brodie reached me.

"And now ye've wrapped me friend around yer finger."

I lowered the revolver.

"Munro is here ..."

He nodded, as he reached out and seized me by the front of my shirt. There was more he would have said, no doubt with a few curses included. Instead, he nodded.

"I know."

And for a moment, just a moment, he pulled me against him.

He was smudged with soot, with faint lines at the corners of his eyes, his hair was wild about his head, and the smell of smoke wrapped around that other faintly scent of spice.

"I'll not ask how ye got here ..."

Only a postponement, I was certain.

"Or, if ye had a thought that ye might be injured?" With a

look down at the outline of the man that lay at the path only a few feet away.

"I saw him at the museum the day Sir Nelson was murdered. He was one of the museum workers."

The distinctive chug of the steam engine as it rolled away from the land and that other man made his escape ended any further argument, if only temporarily. He pushed me away from him and I came up against that other tall Scot.

"There are more just arrived," Munro told him.

I looked at Brodie.

He nodded. "Aye," and turned toward that landing. That dark gaze found me and softened, if only briefly.

"Ye didna think I would come alone."

Then he told Munro, "Get out of here, the both of ye. It's not a place to be when the authorities round up the other others."

"Wait ...!" I called after him

He was gone, as Munro pulled me away from that embankment, away from the gleam of lights that bobbed across the water from other boats that arrived, and the last of that skirmish.

We ran through the cover of trees and up the opposite embankment, as Brown and his men quickly moved ahead toward the wagons.

It might have been a slower ride back across Waterloo Bridge, as we left behind the fire at that ancient watch tower and the myriad smaller lights that invaded the island.

It wasn't, a reminder of those we rode with, Brown and his men who crowded the wagon with us, and the second wagon with more men.

We left the bridge, the night air sharp with the smell of smoke that rode on waves of mist from the river under that sliver of moonlight. The second wagon followed briefly then disappeared down a side road that led farther away.

I leaned against Munro's shoulder in the press of bodies that smelled equally of smoke and the distinctive tang of blood. I glanced at him, and that usually sharp blue gaze was dulled with pain that had returned, no doubt along with the bloodied bandages I would find later. And he was the one to comfort me!

"It's only a wee scratch. I've had worse."

Something Brodie would have said, and had countless times.

It was a wild and often terrifying ride from the river to the Strand, as Brown's men constantly watched for anyone who followed in spite of late hour of the night.

I thought about it afterward, as I put more coal on the fire in the firebox. I had no idea how we managed to reach the Strand without being caught.

It was all a jumble of bodies, as Mr. Cavendish called out orders much like a field commander, I thought, upon our arrival, as he directed Brown's men to take Munro up the stairs to the office. And then my instructions to assist him into the adjacent bedroom.

It was all followed by a blur; they all disappeared from the street below as if they had never been there.

Munro fussed and argued, much like another, as I had him open his shirt and discovered the patch of blood on the bandages.

There followed more grumbling and arguing, as I lit the fire in the firebox, poured steaming water into a basin, and proceeded to remove the bandages.

"I'll not have ye see me naked," he had grumbled again.

I slapped his hand away as I gently cleaned the wound and

applied fresh bandages. It wasn't as if I hadn't seen a man's body before.

"I'd sooner have a dram of whisky," he said in a quiet voice afterward as he buttoned his shirt.

We both had a dram, and waited.

Eighteen

IT WAS VERY near break of day when I heard the door to the office open, and looked up from where I had fallen asleep at Brodie's desk, keeping watch until I could no longer keep my eyes open.

It must have been the whisky. Not to mention that brawl with smugglers, the fire on that narrow island with that abandoned watchtower, and that frantic escape through the streets of London like common criminals.

I still wore clothes from the night before, too exhausted to worry or care, as I insisted that Munro have the bed.

He had argued, and then he hadn't, snoring slightly as I had put more coal on the fire.

And now Brodie was here, smudged with soot and other things that had not been there before, and an expression I had seen at the end of other cases—exhaustion amid the grim reality of death, and I knew without needing to ask.

There was a shadow behind him with a familiar face—Alex Sinclair from the Agency.

That explained a great deal. At the island, Brodie had said he wasn't alone.

Alex, dear young man, with his glasses, that shock of hair that constantly fell over his forehead, his inventions, and obviously a penchant for danger.

He smiled a little shyly in greeting. "I have a new automatic weapon. It worked quite well. It was a spectacular night, Lady Forsythe," he added with enthusiasm, albeit with a bit of confusion as he looked at me and shyly looked away.

"Smugglers and pirates!" he went on. "And it was as if the whole island was afire. You should have been there."

I nodded with a faint smile.

"On yer way," Brodie told him. "And me thanks."

That grin was still there as Alex nodded, bid us both good day, closed the door, and disappeared to the street below.

Brodie smelled of smoke, although whether from the fire on the island or gunpowder it was hard to know.

I went to him, half expecting a lecture. There was none. That would undoubtedly come later.

Or perhaps not, as he lowered his head next to mine, and I felt the weariness as he leaned into me.

"Munro?" he asked.

"Well enough," Munro said, from the doorway to the adjacent room where he had spent the past few hours after more whisky.

"Ye'll live?" Brodie commented to his friend.

"Aye, and saved yer life again," Munro said. "I'm for Sussex Square, where a man isna bothered by troublesome women, and can get some sleep." There was a nod between the old friends that I had seen before.

It was debatable who had saved whose life, but I was not one to argue.

"Good day to the both of ye," Munro said, and then he too was gone.

Brodie's breath was warm against the curve of my neck. His arms tightened round me.

"Ye smell of smoke and whisky, and yerself," he said as he brushed back my hair, buried his face into my shoulder, and simply held on to me before pressing a kiss on my neck.

"And yer covered in soot and grime ... and blood?"

I assured him it was from changing Munro's bandage.

"Yer a grimy baggage, Lady Forsythe. But I'll take ye anyway."

I would have thought it impossible after the night before, exhausted as he must be. He bent down, slipped an arm under my knees, and picked me up. I was not one for such overly romantic gestures that were written about in other novels. However, I would make an exception—or two or three.

"There is one thing," he said as I rested my head against his shoulder and he carried me into that adjacent room.

"Take off yer boots, and dinna wake me for a week or two."

It would be easy enough to say the case was solved. Yet it never was quite that easy. There were so many pieces after that night on the island that still didn't seem to fit.

Yet, as Brodie, who had once been an inspector with the Metropolitan Police and quite accustomed to such things often reminded me ... they were there. It was just a matter of patience, and they began to fall into place.

Motive, means, and opportunity, I thought, as I stared at the chalkboard with the additional notes I had added after that night. They were there as well, a sad, horrifying, and pathetic circumstance that had taken lives and reputations, and very nearly caused an international incident as it played out.

The boat Brodie had followed that night from the island with the assistance of Alex Sinclair and the Agency, put up at Charing Cross pier, where a hired coach waited.

Brodie made light of it afterward. A chase had ensued that made my somewhat frantic ride with Munro and Mr. Brown's men through the streets to the Strand seem like a stroll in the park.

It led from the pier past Parliament to St. James, and to the edge of Grosvenor Square and a stately residence.

Caught and unable to escape after having fled to the columned residence amidst other residences of government officials, barristers, and other respected families, two men were seen in what was an obvious quarrel at the second-floor windows.

As Brodie and others from the Agency attempted to enter, a fire broke out on the second floor and quickly sped, engulfing the entire residence.

The fire brigade arrived, but were turned back, their best efforts required to protect other nearby homes as flames shot into the air.

In the late hours of the day after, the residence had been reduced to ash, charred sandstone, and two bodies that were barely recognizable.

Little else remained except for a rare Egyptian funerary mask found in the wine cellar that suffered only minimal damage, along with a wooden box with ancient Egyptian carvings.

The residence had belonged to Sir Anthony Fellowes, and yet another piece fell into place. His charred body was one that was found, the other presumably that of the smuggler, Duvalier. Though it was impossible to know for certain.

It only raised more questions, which were answered in the days that followed, as Brodie and I accompanied Alex and others from the Agency to the warehouse where I had last spoken with Sir Anthony.

There, in a sub-floor chamber that might never have been discovered if not for that night on the island, a horde of other Egyptian artifacts were discovered.

An international incident arose over the stolen antiquities, followed by that demand the Egyptian counsel had made for all artifacts to be returned. He had submitted a document Sir Nelson had signed, for the '*loan*' of the items in the exhibit at the museum, with everything to be returned once the exhibit closed.

The discovery of that stolen shipment aboard the steamship after Sir Anthony fled the island, along with the horde hidden at the warehouse, ignited a furor over claimants to the artifacts.

Egypt was a Crown colony, yet Britain's presence there required a delicate balancing act, as I had witnessed on my earlier travels.

As for Sir Anthony Fellowes' motive?

That close friendship from their school days had waned considerably as Sir Nelson received accolades from many academics and royal patrons, as well as financial backing for his next trip back to Egypt. Another piece discovered, as a university fellow who read the account in the dailies, came forward to mourn the deaths of his colleagues.

He spoke of the fierce competitiveness on the part of Sir Anthony Fellowes. It seemed that envy over the years fed his bitterness, and apparently led to the murder of Sir Nelson and

Mr. Hosni over the accolades which Fellowes felt might have been his.

Greed and envy led him to an encounter with a man who worked at the museum—a man with a limp in his left leg, and the same man who had attacked me and taken the wooden box from the exhibit, and then died on the island.

Duvalier's part in all of it was that of procurer, simply stated: a smuggler with connections in vast parts of Europe and a network of thieves who lived in the shadows but were skilled at acquiring valuable works of art and ancient artifacts for a price.

He had the ability and the skill to bring a shipment out of Egypt to private buyers in London, including that smuggled shipment Brodie and Munro had followed from Portsmouth.

It did seem that Sophie Marquette was an innocent victim in all of this, except for the poor choice of Duvalier. They were to have met at Dover after he completed his latest 'business' transaction, according to that note I found. In a small way, I felt sorry for her.

Mr. Brown had played his part as well and would undoubtedly want to collect on that favor owed; however, that was a piece in all of this best left for another time. Considering the man's reputation, it was not a comforting thought. Still, I had to admit, somewhat grudgingly, that he had provided both valuable information and assistance that might have ended far differently.

John Sutcliffe was sent word of his uncle's death and subsequent funeral. There was no response.

It was sad that his relationship with his uncle, who was a very fine man, had been reduced to monetary value.

With the experience that I gained over the past three years since that first inquiry case with Brodie, and from my own personal history, I knew there were some things that could never be resolved.

One simply had to live with them and move on, as my great aunt had once told me. Obsessing over a thing that was over and done was a senseless waste of one's time.

"I live by that," she said at the time. *"As far as anyone knows, we only have so much time in this life, and none of it should be wasted on things that cannot be changed. Although,"* she had added, *"I do have plans on returning after I'm gone from this life. Perhaps as a sea otter. They are marvelous little creatures, quite jolly and carefree."*

Anyone else who heard the conversation at the time would undoubtedly have decided that she was becoming quite dotty, yet I knew different, and had spent the past years since she took my sister and me to live with her, attempting to follow by example. It was something that flummoxed Brodie from time to time.

"Ye are just like her. I dinna know if the world is safe."

Other pieces in our investigation came together. New lists were made of artifacts discovered in that hidden room below the warehouse, along with those found aboard the boat that Duvalier had used to smuggle in that shipment from Portsmouth.

There were dozens of statues, gold-inlaid bowls, Coptic jars, funerary masks, and jewelry that were to be displayed in the exhibit. The Egyptian counsel had already submitted a written request that it was *all* to be returned, along with the original artifacts Sir Nelson had found and collected.

I was as fascinated and intrigued by those ancient artifacts as so many others were. Yet, I felt a certain sadness as I had on one of my travels to Egypt, when I had watched artifacts like those in the exhibit, collected from ancient burial sites, then sold in marketplaces and carried aboard ship for a journey to another country, to be put on display like trophies.

The Egyptian counsel had made several more appeals that were being considered. I, for one, thought all of the artifacts should be returned, most particularly funerary relics.

As for that small wooden box with those ancient carvings found with other artifacts in that room under the warehouse floor, it somehow mysteriously disappeared amid the arguing and confusion over the ownership of the artifacts.

"Ye are a thief," Brodie exclaimed when he discovered the box in the office on the Strand.

That did seem a bit like splitting hairs, given his somewhat colorful past.

"A simple wooden box," I pointed out. "I am simply returning it to the rightful owner, since no one seems capable of making a decision about the artifacts. And you have never taken something?"

"It's a different thing when a child is starving to death," he replied with a frown.

"A coin pinched when said child is running numbers for a local gambling club?" I inquired of one of the stories from that childhood. "Or perhaps a gentleman's watch lifted from his pocket?"

"That was a long time ago, and ye know better." He made a sound. "My wife is a thief."

"I do believe in keeping things in the family," I replied, which brought another typically Scottish sound I had become quite familiar with.

I had placed a telephone call to my great aunt at Sussex Square. She knew a great many people, including the English Ambassador to Egypt, who was presently in England and had found himself swept up in the issue over the stolen artifacts.

"Of course, dear. I shall send round a message to Sidney and have him arrange a meeting for you with the Egyptian counsel."

Easily said and done. There were times when I did question who was actually Queen of England.

Not surprisingly, the meeting was arranged very soon after. Brodie made no comment as I set off for that meeting with that carved cedar box in my travel bag.

Adnan Sharif was the official counsel from his country to the Court of St. James. Through him, delicate and often politically fraught issues as a Crown colony were brought, and resolution attempted.

He was an older man, who had been educated in England and had returned to Egypt in the years after. He had no official office, but met diplomats and other officials at his residence in Kensington.

He was said to be highly intelligent, shrewd, and a master in the art of negotiation.

We had never met, but I had heard of him through my great aunt.

"*A handsome devil,*" she declared. "*And said to be from one of the richest families in Egypt.*"

His residence, I discovered, in spite of the fact that he held no formal title, was very much like an embassy, with an arched entrance, and an attendant in traditional Egyptian attire who rose from a desk and bowed his head in greeting.

The Counsel Sharif had agreed to meet with me through a written message to Aunt Antonia.

He rose from behind his own desk as his secretary, also in traditional Egyptian attire that men wore, made him aware that I had arrived.

Instead of the long white *thawb* and traditional headdress

his attendants wore, he wore a suit of clothes that an English gentleman might have worn. He bowed his head in greeting and I thanked him for meeting with me.

"Lady Forsythe, you are most welcome. I am pleased to make your acquaintance."

I was familiar with the Egyptian language and accent, along with that reserved demeanor, from past encounters on my travels. The Counsel was polite and articulate, yet I sensed that shrewdness my great aunt had spoken of.

"I was somewhat surprised by Lady Montgomery's request, considering the present difficult situation between our two countries regarding stolen Egyptian artifacts," he said as he returned to his chair behind the desk. I took the chair opposite as his assistant remained beside the door, silent but watchful.

Two countries.

It was not lost on me that the Counsel referred to Egypt as a separate country, even after past conflicts with Britain, a war, and now that protective status.

I explained that I was there with the hope of perhaps easing that difficulty between the two in some small way.

"How might that be?" he politely responded.

As I stood and reached for my travel bag on the floor, I caught the sudden movement from his assistant. The Counsel shook his head and waved him back. It was a reminder that although he might be welcomed by the British government, there might be dangers, those who promoted conflict.

I placed the bag on the chair, then retrieved the cedar box that I had 'appropriated' from the artifacts that were discovered in Sir Anthony's possession. I set it on the desk before Counsel Sharif.

In spite of that reserved demeanor when I had first arrived, I noticed the way his eyes sharpened.

"This was originally displayed at the museum," I explained. "It was among the artifacts Sir Nelson had brought back for the exhibit."

That dark gaze was fastened on the box.

"I don't know what the markings mean, but it is apparently of some importance."

Counsel Sharif looked up. He reached across the desk for the box.

"It is very old," he said as he gently held the cedar box. "The markings on the box are for protection for what it contains." He gently set the box back on the desk, and almost reverently lifted the gold clasp that secured the lid.

He sat back in his desk chair with a startled expression.

"It is over two thousand years old and was thought to be lost forever," he said as he gazed at the contents, then carefully removed what appeared to be a scroll.

With equal care he set it on the desk beside the box. It appeared to be made of papyrus wrapped around a small cedar staff.

He bowed his head and whispered in that ancient language. His assistant did the same. Counsel Sharif looked up.

"You must forgive me. You could not have known. It is only that this is of far more value to my people than gold."

He explained that it was an ancient 'manuscript' of magical spells and prayers, written by priests centuries before to accompany the dead into the afterlife.

Stories about the scroll had been handed down through those centuries, but it was thought the scroll was lost to the sands of time.

He smiled for the first time.

"It is with some irony that it was found by those who have

taken so much from my people, and that you have now returned it.

"I must believe that the words carved on the box have protected the scroll all this time."

"Much like an amulet?" I said, and explained that Mr. Hosni had given me his own for protection.

I had carried it the entire time we searched for that smuggled cargo, and still did so. I retrieved it from the pocket of my gown.

When I would have given it to Counsel Sharif as well, he held up a hand.

"It was given for protection. You must keep it; it kept you safe and guided you to find the box."

I wasn't certain that I believed in such things, although my friend, Templeton, would have argued that.

"Will there be difficulty for you because you brought me this?" he asked as I stood to leave.

Brodie had called me a thief, if a well-intentioned one. I looked upon it differently.

"I simply honored Sir Nelson's agreement that the artifacts were to be returned No one specified when that might be done," I replied and then left.

Afterward, I returned to the office on the Strand.

In the days that followed, the pieces were all finally there. I sat at my typing machine, pecking away, as Brodie called it. There was that report of our inquiry, which Sir Avery with the Agency insisted upon. Even though Brodie had met with him several times to 'brief' him, as he called it, on the developments of the case.

There had been quite a stir in the dailies about the smuggled artifacts, following Sir Nelson's murder. It had included mention of the arrest of a 'certain prominent person of notable family' in the matter in an article written by Theodolphus Burke with the Times of London.

Although no names were mentioned—I was waiting for 'the other shoe to drop,' something my friend Templeton had said once from her travels to New York when on tour. It did seem most appropriate.

Burke—I refused to dignify the man by calling him Mr. Burke—had the reputation for name dropping, salacious gossip, and dropping carefully edited information that failed to mention actual details, merely to cause a sensation.

Not that I was concerned in the matter. It was simply irritating that such a man considered himself a journalist, with his sly habits meant to increase his journalistic standing, not to mention the readership of the Times.

Over luncheon recently with Templeton, she had suggested contacting Mr. Shakespeare in the matter.

"He is quite fond of you, you know."

I didn't and was highly suspicious what that might mean.

"I have discovered that he has very unusual ways of expressing himself," she continued. "Have I mentioned that my fellow actor, Mr. Price, who cannot act his way out of a bag, has recently found himself with a debilitating injury? It seems that his understudy—a delicious young man—will be replacing him." And she smiled.

Brodie simply shook his head when I told him about it.

"The woman is addled, and Munro is well rid of her."

She might well be, but she was a dear friend, and I wasn't as certain that Munro was well rid of her, or the way round.

Our report had been submitted to Sir Avery at the Agency,

and there had been additional meetings which I handily avoided. The less involvement with the Agency, the better, as far as I was concerned. Yet, I had my suspicions on that.

As the furor over Sir Nelson's murder lessened and life settled back into what I considered normal, Brodie and I made plans to close the office and escape north to Scotland.

There were rumblings of influenza as the weather warmed, confirmed by Mr. Brimley. Aunt Antonia had already departed with most of her household, which included Munro, who had fully recovered.

I had asked Mrs. Ryan if she cared to accompany us.

"The place full of Scots?" she had exclaimed and promptly departed for a visit with her sister's family 'just over the way' in Ireland. I didn't bother to tell her that a good part of Ireland had been settled by Scots in the past.

Mr. Cavendish had scoffed at the idea of leaving for a time. Where would he go? He had been to many ports in his time at sea, exposed to all sorts of 'miseries,' as he called them, and saw no reason to leave. And there was a reason to remain, to watch over the office with the hound and keep an eye on a particular woman at the Public House.

With arrangements more or less made for our pending departure, I had met with James Warren, my publisher, who also happened to be my brother-in-law.

He and Linnie were soon departing for Brighton for a few weeks. He was seeing to last details for the publishing house.

"I've been thinking," he said, something I was familiar with, over coffee at the Grand Hotel very near the rail station that would take Brodie and me to Inverness and on to Old Lodge in the next few days.

"Your Emma books," as he called them, referring to my novels with my heroine Emma Fortescue. "They have been extraordinarily successful. Far more so than anyone's expectations. And the last one with that bit of a mystery that you had her go off and solve, the sales have been quite astounding.

"It does seem as if your readers are eager for more mystery and murder, far different than the bare statistics they read in the crime sheets.

"I know you have little time for taking yourself off on your foreign adventures with the inquiry cases you take with Mr. Brodie. Yet, Emma Fortescue is such a fascinating character, and those self-defense moves you write about fascinate readers.

"Have you considered writing another mystery? Perhaps a series of them?"

Author Note

The late 19th century and early 20th century was a time for enormous exploration beyond Britain.

There were several noted explorers, Howard Carter among them. He's a young man just starting out, for the sake of the story, but fascinated by Egypt and eager to begin his own travels. Later in the 20th century, he becomes famous for the discovery of the nearly complete tomb of Tutankhamun, the boy king. And as they say, the rest is history.

The 19th century was a time of tumult and discovery in Egypt. Britain fought a war over it and the vast riches to be found there. It eventually became a protectorate of Britain, then an independent country years later.

The loss of artifacts through the decades was considered nothing more than pillaging in the name of exploration. Many artifacts were smuggled out of the country and made their way into private collections, as well as museums.

Some have found their way back to Egypt and been added to artifacts discovered more recently by archeologists who have established their own antiquities department, with the hope of preserving their history.

Sir William Flinders-Petrie was a British archeologist and pioneered the sequence-dating method that has allowed others to more accurately date artifacts that are discovered in England and other parts of the world.

I used the smell of the spice absinthe as a means of identifying a particular person. In addition, I used the 'limp' early on as one of those small clues sprinkled along the way regarding the potential murderer.

As for other points of possible interest:

The portable typewriter that Brodie purchased for Mikaela was invented in the late 19th century by W.P. Laidlaw of Glasgow. A Scot of all things.

I researched railway travel in Britain extensively. The routes and time between points are from actual railway schedules for the period.

I also researched the schedule for both high and low tides at various times of the year for the River Thames, as close as possible to the time period.

There are several islands in the river. Most are in the north and now home to private residences. For the sake of the story, I created that narrow slip of land with that watchtower from Roman times where the smuggled cargo was taken.

Fashions had changed somewhat as the new century approached. Women now wore blouses with skirts, introduced by the French. Even though Mikaela has been known from time to time to prefer trousers, jumpers (sweaters), and boots when out and about investigating a crime.

She does have a habit of getting herself into the middle of things, and it was quite entertaining for me to have her 'arrested' when found at the scene of a murder. Of course, there was Brodie's reaction, which surprisingly did not end in a lecture about putting herself in danger.

And finally, the Hole in the Wall tavern where Brodie meets with Mr. Dodge, who tells him where he delivered that smuggled cargo.

I couldn't resist. It is a real pub.

The original Hole in the Wall tavern was built in 1612 in Bowness and mentioned by Charles Dickens. The name came from an actual hole in the wall of the pub through which a workman was handed a glass of beer from time to time as he worked.

Another Hole in the Wall Tavern is very near Waterloo Rail Station at 5 Mepham Street, London, under the arch that I have described, where one can find a pint of craft beer and perhaps a dram.

Brodie and Mikaela are off to Scotland after an outbreak of influenza in London. But there is that suggestion from her publisher about writing another murder mystery.

Hmmm ... So many stories to write, so many murders.

Including one from the past, with a letter that finds Mikaela at Old Lodge in Scotland that will challenge her and bring her up against the secrets of the past from her own childhood, while Brodie is drawn back into the intrigues of the Agency.

Coming next

DEADLY GHOSTS

Betrayed

Revenge

Outlaws, Scoundrels & Lawmen

Desperado's Caress

Passion's Splendor

Silver Mistress

Memory and Desire

Desire's Flame

Silken Surrender

Angels, Devils, Rebels & Rogues

Ravished

Always My Love

Seductive Caress

Seduced

Deceived

"I want to write a book …" she said.

"Then do it," he said.

And she did, and received two offers for that first book proposal.

A dozen historical romances later, and a prophecy from a gifted psychic and the Legacy Series was created, expanding to seven additional titles.

Along the way, two film options, and numerous book awards.

But wait, there's more a voice whispered, after a trip to Scotland and a visit to the standing stones in the far north, and as old as Stonehenge, sign posts the voice told her, and the Clan Fraser books that have followed that told the beginnings of the clan and the family she was part of …

And now … murder and mystery set against the backdrop of Victorian London in the new Angus Brodie and Mikaela Forsythe series, with an assortment of conspirators and murderers in the brave new world after the Industrial Revolution where terrorists threaten and the world spins closer to war.

When she is not exploring the Darkness of the fantasy world, or pursuing ancestors in ancient Scotland, she lives in the mountains near Yosemite National Park with bears and mountain lions, and plots murder and revenge.

And did I mention fierce, beautiful women and dangerous, handsome men?

They're there, waiting ...

Join Carla's Newsletter

www.ingramcontent.com/pod-product-compliance
Lightning Source LLC
Chambersburg PA
CBHW050311110726
47899CB00007B/2195